The Loser's Guide to Life and Love

THE LOSER'S GUIDE TO LIFE AND LOVE

A NOVEL

A. E. Cannon

HARPER TEEN

An Imprint of HarperCollins*Publishers*

HarperTeen is an imprint of HarperCollins Publishers.

The Loser's Guide to Life and Love
Copyright © 2008 by A. E. Cannon
www.harperteen.com

Library of Congress Cataloging-in-Publication Data
Cannon, A. E. (Ann Edwards)
    The loser's guide to life and love / A. E. Cannon. — 1st ed.
        p.   cm.
    Summary: Over the summer, Salt Lake City high school student Ed
McIff works at the video store wearing a name tag with the name
Sergio on it, and when a beautiful new girl comes into the store, he
decides to take on a new, more suave identity, resulting in a series
of misunderstandings and star-crossed encounters.
    ISBN 978-0-06-112846-2 (trade bdg.) — ISBN 978-0-06-112847-9
(lib. bdg.)
    [1. Identity—Fiction. 2. Interpersonal relations—Fiction. 3. Salt
Lake City (Utah)—Fiction.] I. Title.
PZ7.C17135Lo 2008   2007020850
[Fic]—dc22   CIP
                                                                   AC

Typography by Amy Ryan
1 2 3 4 5 6 7 8 9 10

First Edition

For Betsy Burton, with affection and respect

I want to acknowledge the help given me by the following individuals—

My gifted editor, Catherine Onder, who whipped Ed (a.k.a. Sergio) into shape;

My agent, Tracey Adams, for taking me on and finding the best of all possible homes for my manuscript;

My great friend Louise Plummer, for shoring me up when the waters turned rough;

My coworkers at The King's English Bookshop, for inspiring me with their smarts;

My brother Jimmy, for not giving up hope;

My second oldest son, Alec, who taught me how to say thanks in Portuguese;

My oldest son, Phil, who slicked back his hair and gave me the idea;

My best friend of thirty summers and counting, Ken Cannon—

Without these grand people this book would have never seen the light of day (let alone a midsummer's eve).

The poet's eye, in a fine frenzy rolling,
Doth glance from heaven to earth,
    from earth to heaven;
And, as imagination bodies forth
The forms of things unknown, the poet's pen
Turns them to shapes, and gives to airy nothing
A local habitation and a name.

—William Shakespeare,
A Midsummer Night's Dream

On June 21st

You and a guest of your choice

are invited to attend

A Midsummer Eve's Celebration

From dusk to dawn

at the midnight-blue, mosaic-covered house

of Ali and his Warrior Princess

1001 Fourth Avenue

In the City

Beneath the Moon

JUNE 12

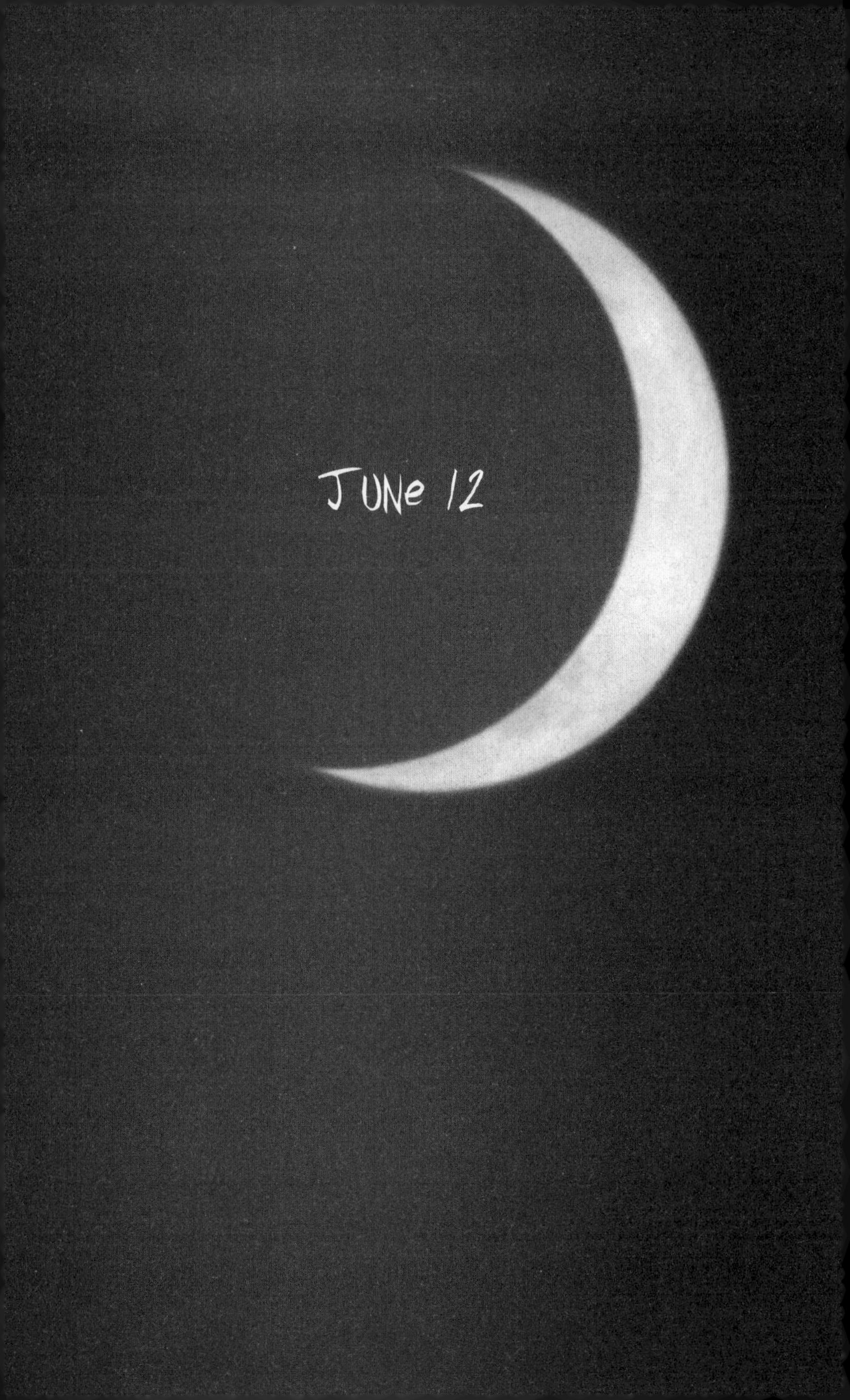

ED'S TURN

"You look like a total dork, Ed," says my eight-year-old sister, the Lovely and Talented Maggie McIff, as I prepare to go to work at Reel Life Movies.

She has looked up from her unnaturally large pile of nude Barbie dolls long enough to make this encouraging observation, and as I catch a glimpse of myself in the entryway mirror, I have to agree (silently) that she is right. Let me make this quick director's note, however: Even if you were a movie star, you TOO would look like a dork if you were required to wear shiny wingtips, black tuxedo pants, a red cummerbund, a white frilly shirt, and snappy red bow tie to work. Reel Life employees are supposed to look like old-fashioned ushers at a place like

Grauman's Chinese Theatre in Hollywood, although most of our customers say we look like Chippendale dancers.

Just not as chiseled.

It also does not help that I have to wear a former Reel Life employee's name tag because my boss (that would be the incredibly intimidating Ali) hasn't made me a new one even though I've been working for three weeks now. The strange thing is that Ali is usually all over this kind of detail. Everybody knows he's the most organized and efficient manager in the whole entire history of the video and DVD rental industry.

Makes you wonder what's going on, doesn't it?

Anyway, my friend and fellow coworker Scout Arrington helped me land the job because she knows I love movies as much as she does. In fact, here's a confession: I want to make movies of my own one day.

DO NOT LAUGH.

It could happen. I could be the next Steven Spielberg. Somebody has to be.

Right now, however, I am just an ordinary, boring sixteen-year-old guy named Ed McIff with a name tag that says "Sergio."

Sergio?

Scout says "Sergio" sounds like the name of a romantic male lead in a daytime soap.

"Well, that would definitely make me the Anti-Sergio,"

I tell her, because (frankly) I am NOT the kind of guy women have fantasies about. For one thing, I'm short.

"Tom Cruise isn't that big of a guy," my mom always says. I love how she tries to avoid using the word "short."

"Yeah," I tell her in return, "but he compensates by being Tom Cruise." Not that anyone really wants to BE Tom Cruise anymore now that he's a crazy couch jumper. But whatever.

I check the entryway mirror one more time. Yup. I'm still short.

"You usually look like a dork," the Lovely and Talented Maggie McIff adds for clarification purposes, "but tonight you look dorkier than usual because your hair is sticking up." She serenely braids beads into the hair of one of her bare-naked Barbie dolls.

"Thank you very much," I say. "Now how would YOU like it if I borrowed Quark's junior chemistry set and blew up all your Barbie dolls while you're asleep tonight?"

Quark (short for Quentin Andrews O'Rourke) is our next-door neighbor. We're exactly the same age—we were even born on the same day and used to have our birthday parties together when we were little—but that's where the resemblance ends. He's a braniac who goes to a private high school for certified geniuses somewhere out in Sandy, a community south of Salt Lake City, where we live.

Quark is also a genius who happens to look EXACTLY like Brad Pitt, in spite of the fact that he a) rarely combs his hair and b) gets mixed up when it comes to putting on matching clothes. He's freakishly tall, though, so I guess you could say he looks like Brad Pitt would if B. P. were suffering from some rare movie-star glandular disorder.

Quark, however, has absolutely no idea that he's good-looking, and he wouldn't care anyway, because Quark lives for the thrill of scientific investigation.

The Lovely and Talented's big eyes grow bigger.

"You wouldn't dare blow up my Barbies," she cries, gathering them up like a mother hen gathering up her chicks. Or however that cliché goes.

"Do not push me," I warn her, looking into the mirror one last time. "I'm one of those walking human time bombs"—speaking of clichés!—"ready to explode."

"It's almost six," Mom calls to me from the kitchen. "Time to be at work, Ed."

"I'm on my way," I shout back.

"See you later . . . *Sergio*," she trills at me. Then she bursts into gales of maniacal laughter, not unlike a mad scientist.

Is it just me, or do you also think this is unnatural behavior in a female parent? Isn't there a federal law on the books that says mothers are not allowed to laugh at vulnerable male children when they are required to wear stupid clothing to work?

There should be.

I open our ordinary, boring front door and let myself out into another ordinary, boring summer night.

On my way to work (I'm driving my mother's highly pathetic vintage Geo), I write the following script in my head, which is something I like to do when things get slow. I'm thinking this might make an interesting documentary for PBS. What's your opinion?

The Ordinary, Boring Life
of a Typical American Youth Called Ed
Being an (un)original screenplay by Ed McIff

The camera zooms in on an average sixteen-year-old American boy wearing flannel boxers and sitting on a bar stool, wondering if he should start working out at the gym with his friend Scout. This intense mental activity has left him feeling somewhat weak. Also hungry.

ANNOUNCER GUY:

(who sounds like Prince Charles, only snootier) Greetings to all our highly intelligent viewers at home! Today we are going to meet an average sixteen-year-old American lad. You there, laddie!

ED:

(looking around to see where the strange voice is coming from as he does his best Robert De Niro imitation) Are you talking to me? Are YOU talking to ME?

ANNOUNCER GUY:

Indeed, I am! Your name, please?

ED:

Ed McIff.

ANNOUNCER GUY:

Tell us something about yourself, Ed.

ED:

Well, there's not a lot to tell—

ANNOUNCER GUY:

Come now! You don't want to disappoint our broad-minded and politically correct viewers who support this and other programs on their local public television stations, do you?

ED:

I don't know. I never thought about it before.

ANNOUNCER GUY:

Why don't you share some of your likes and dislikes with us? For instance, what foreign country have you most enjoyed visiting?

ED:

Does Disneyland count?

ANNOUNCER GUY:

(sounding annoyed although still polite) Let's try this again, shall we? What's your favorite Shakespearean play?

ED:

To tell you the truth, I think Shakespeare is kind of lame. All those goofy plays about people passing themselves off as other people. Pretty stupid, don't you think?

ANNOUNCER GUY:

(sounding huffy and no longer polite) Well! This is certainly going nowhere in a very big hurry. All right then, Mr. McIff. I've got a request that surely even YOU can handle. Describe your typical summer day for us.

ED:

Okay. I wake up about eleven or twelve, because I stayed up late working at Reel Life the night before with Scout and Ali and sometimes T. Monroe Menlove. Then I go into the kitchen and pour myself a big bowl of cold cereal.

Lucky Charms.

After I eat, I sit on the couch in my boxers and flip through television talk shows for a while so I can watch big, trashy girls fight with each other while their tattoo-covered boyfriends look on.

After that I shower, get dressed, and go to my neighbor Quark's house for the afternoon, where I play video games while he tells me about the exciting moon phenomena he observed through his trusty telescope the night before. Quark knows more about the moon than even real live astronauts do.

Anyway, after that I come back home and bug my sister, Maggie, and after that I change into my work clothes and go to Reel Life, where I work until two a.m.

ANNOUNCER GUY:

And that's it? That's all you do, day after day after day?

ED:

Well, sometimes I have Cap'n Crunch with crunchberries for breakfast. I love crunchberries. And of course I change my boxers every morning because that's just the kind of guy I am! *(Ed says this part with obvious pride.)*

ANNOUNCER GUY:

You seriously mean to tell us you have nothing else in your life? No girlfriends?

ED:

Whoa! Wait a minute! No need to get personal, pal. It's tough to get out and meet girls when you're a short guy who works nights in a frilly girly-man shirt.

ANNOUNCER GUY:

Mr. McIff, did anybody ever tell you you're a loser?

Cut!

Okay. You're absolutely right. A script like this will never fly on PBS. A script about Sergio, on the other hand, just might be the ticket.

Scout and I like to wonder about the mysterious former employee Sergio, whose badge I wear and whom no one—not even T. Monroe Menlove, who's been at Reel Life forever—seems to remember. Who was he? Why did he leave Reel Life? Where is he now? Making up things about Sergio is one of our favorite pastimes.

"I think his extremely wealthy family in Brazil must have called and said it was time for him to come home," Scout always starts off.

"To oversee their vast plantation," I say.

"Because they miss him and need him, and they're tired of him traveling all over the globe," she says.

"Surfing off the coast of Australia," I say.

"Hunting tigers in India," she says.

"Racing Formula One cars and frolicking with topless princesses in Monaco," I say.

"Riding camels in Egypt," she says.

"Hiking in the Himalayas," I say.

"Working at Reel Life in Salt Lake City just because

he feels like slumming for a while," she says.

"And how does Sergio react to the news that he must return to the family plantation in Brazil?" I ask.

"He stays calm. Sergio is always cool, even in the face of disappointment. Or danger," says Scout.

"In fact, Sergio laughs in the face of danger," I point out. "Ha! Ha! Ha!"

"He laughs, it's true. But he does not sweat. Sergio never sweats," she says.

"And even if he did, it would be a completely good kind of sweat," I say.

"A very manly sweat," says Scout.

Then Scout and I look at each other and laugh, which causes T. Monroe (our resident born-again Christian) to remind us that the Lord disapproves of light-mindedness.

Sergio. Sergio. Wherefore art thou Sergio?

I switch my hands on the steering wheel of my mother's Geo (the real Sergio wouldn't be caught dead driving this car, BTW) and smile to myself.

Man, how good would it feel to be Sergio?

"Late!" Ali booms at me as I sail through the door of Reel Life. He's standing with his arms folded across his chest like the world's hugest genie. "Third time this month, baby."

He's probably glaring at me, but it's hard to tell because Ali always wears black wraparound sunglasses. Even inside. Even at night.

I make a quick apology, experiencing my usual feelings for Ali of respect and total mind-numbing fear. At six feet ten inches and three hundred pounds of granite-solid muscle, Ali is a Tower of Terror. Rumor has it that he goes to Vegas and picks up a little extra cash now and then as an ultimate fighter.

He's never been beaten, people say. The man's a legend. A freakin' myth.

I join Scout at the checkout station, and she lands a friendly punch on my arm.

"Slacker! I think you're just trying to get yourself fired so you won't have to invite someone to Ali's Midsummer Eve's party."

I groan.

"Hey, relax. You're not required to bring a date." Scout starts stacking a truckload of DVDs someone has just returned. "Ali says you can bring anybody you want to—a friend, a family member, a complete stranger if necessary. T. Monroe is taking his mother."

"Excuse me," I say, "but who wants to be like T. Monroe? Anyway, I already invited Quark to go with me." I sigh. You would too, if you were me and Quark was your date.

Here's the deal. Ali and his girlfriend, the Warrior Princess, throw a huge, very famous party every June 21. They invite everybody they know with the request that all guests bring someone. It's supposed to be the best party ever. Even T. Monroe, who's absolutely no fun at all, goes slack-jawed with joy whenever he remembers last year's party.

So I've been invited to Ali's costume ball because I'm a new employee here at Reel Life. Only I don't really want to go. Here are my reasons.

First, Ali makes me nervous. I always feel like he's *testing* me somehow, and while I don't think I've exactly failed this mysterious test yet, I'm pretty sure I haven't passed it, either.

Second, I don't know what to do for a costume.

Third, I can see myself showing up with Quark and finding out that everybody else there really does have a date. Ha! Gotcha again, McIff, they'll all say.

"Who did you invite, Scout?" I want to know.

"No one yet." She shrugs, not worried.

"Too bad we can't take each other to the party," I joke.

Now here comes the weird part. Scout blushes.

"Sorry if I scared you," I add in a hurry.

Scout waves this away but doesn't say anything, which makes me feel even worse. You know things are bad when one of your best friends doesn't want to be seen in public at a party with you.

I glance over at Ali, who is busy in the other checkout stand entertaining some customers—an older woman with two little girls in pink and orange dresses with paper flowers in their blue-black hair. Ali is full of secret smiles and shifty moves as he performs one of his many magic tricks. This time he asks for the woman's driver's license. She hands it over to him and he makes it disappear into thin air.

Poof!

And suddenly he pulls it out from behind one of the little girls' ears.

The three of them squeal with delight and clap their hands.

"Ali," Scout says with an admiring grin, "is just the greatest!"

Time flies on a busy summer night at Reel Life when you're working with Scout. I'm surprised that it's time for us to take our late-night dinner break.

"Wanna go across the street to Smith's Marketplace with me?" I ask as we walk out the door together. "I need to buy a Barbie."

A couple of skaters passing us on their way inside hear me. "Whoa! Did you just hear that?" they say to each other. "The freakin' dude in the frilly shirt just said he needs to buy himself a freakin' Barbie."

Scout blurts out a laugh.

"Hey, losers," I shout at them over my shoulder, "it's for my sister, okay?"

Then I explain things to Scout. "I kind of scared the Lovely and Talented tonight before I left the house. The least I can do is buy her a freakin' Barbie doll."

Overhead the moon is high and bright.

"You're a good big brother, Ed," Scout says as we pick our way across the busy street. "You're just like my big brother, Ben."

Ben, who's nineteen, lives somewhere in the jungles of northern Brazil, dodging big bugs and fish that eat people. He's serving a two-year mission for the Mormon Church, and even though Scout gets to drive his very fine powder blue '69 Mustang convertible while he's gone, she misses him like crazy.

"Moons like this always make me think of Ben," Scout says. "Sometimes when he sees the moon he repeats the last lines from a poem our mom used to read to us. 'Hand in hand, on the edge of the sand, they danced by the light of the moon, the moon, the moon. They danced by the light of the moon.' I wonder if Ben's figured out how to say that in Portuguese yet."

"I used to wish on the moon," I tell Scout. "My dad told me I should wish on a star, but I liked the moon better because it was bigger. I figured that way my wishes had a better chance of coming true."

Scout laughed. "Guys! Bigger is always better. So what are you wishing for tonight, Ed McIff?"

"Nothing. It doesn't work, so I don't bother anymore."

This is only partially true. Wishing on the moon does NOT work, which I know from direct personal experience. But I do it anyway. Almost every single night. And what I wish for tonight as I set out to buy my sister another freakin' Barbie doll is that my life weren't so ordinary. And boring.

I wish that magic would strike and set everything on fire.

So anyway, Scout and I end up buying the Lovely and Talented a new NASCAR Barbie because Barbie is so very liberated these days, she can even drive her own hot pink race car, thank you very much. Then we return to Reel Life, where Ali tells us to shelve DVDs, which is precisely what I'm doing now.

I'm in the foreign film section, wondering why, in fact, anybody would want to sit through a movie they had to read. I put *Diva* on the shelf.

Someone taps me on the shoulder. "Excuse me. Do you work here?"

If I were braver, I would give this question the answer it so richly deserves: *Of course not! I simply enjoy prancing around town in tuxedo pants and a cummerbund for the sheer thrill of it all!*

One thing you learn real fast when you enter the work force and start dealing with the American public is just how many people there are who CANNOT WAIT TO ASK YOU A STUPID QUESTION.

"Yes," I answer politely as I tuck another DVD back

onto the shelf. Then I turn around to face the asker of the stupid question.

And discover standing before me a goddess on a seashell, just like in that old Italian painting.

Okay. Maybe she doesn't look exactly like Aphrodite shooting the curl on a half shell. For one thing, the girl standing in front of me this very minute isn't naked.

Trust me. I would notice if she were.

She is, however, the closest thing I have seen to a Greek goddess in the city of Salt Lake. Here is a short descriptive list:

Blond of hair.

Brown of eye.

Full of lip.

Smooth of skin.

Long of leg.

You just look at this girl and think she's so much higher up on the food chain than you are that the two of you don't even belong to the same species. And for the record, this is exactly the kind of girl who is never interested in dorks wearing red cummerbunds. Dorks like me, for example.

She flashes me a dazzling smile (her teeth, I'm sure you'll be thrilled to learn, are white and even, not unlike a strand of fine pearls). Then, looking at my name tag, she says, "You're Sergio? What a very cool name!"

My heart begins to pound beneath my frilly white

shirt. Here it is. Magic striking. My big break. I've been discovered. *YES!!*

"Yes. Indeed," I say, barely believing what I hear coming out of my own mouth. "That would be me. I am Sergio. Sergio Mendes."

Behind me, Scout drops a load of DVDs, which clatter to the floor. Meanwhile, I wonder what tiny corner of my brain the name "Mendes" came from. I have to admit it does have a vaguely familiar ring.

"Wow!" the Amazingly Beautiful Girl says, and I can tell that she's interested. In me! "Sergio Mendes. Are you from somewhere besides Salt Lake City originally?"

I can feel Scout's eyeballs boring tiny little holes into my back.

"Yes," I say *muy* brightly, marveling how easy it is to tell this girl lies. "I am from Brazil originally."

Scout sounds the way my dad did that time he nearly choked on a pastrami Big H burger at Hires Restaurant, and Jim, the manager, had to perform the Heimlich maneuver on him.

The Beautiful Girl looks past me and focuses on Scout, concern written across her face. "Are you all right?" she asks Scout.

"I'm fine," Scout says.

"You're sure?"

Scout nods, her face still red.

"Well, okay then," the Beautiful Girl says, still looking

at Scout. She pauses, searching for something to say. "Isn't it great that Sergio here is from Brazil? He's all the way from Brazil, but he speaks English like a native!"

"Like a pure native," Scout agrees. "I'll bet he speaks *Brazilian* like a pure native, too." Scout sounds a little too snide. Is she going to blow my cover?

"Brazilian?" The Beautiful Girl gives this some serious thought. "Well, you're probably right."

Scout snorts and starts picking up DVDs.

The Beautiful Girl turns her attention back to me and wraps her long arms around herself as she sighs dreamily. "I've never been anywhere. Just living here in Salt Lake with my aunt Mary this summer is such a huge big deal for me. And I really love it here, you guys. Honest! The mountains turn blue just before the sun goes down. At home the hills are red. Always red."

"Where's home?" I (the socially appropriate Sergio) ask.

"Santa Clara in southern Utah," she answers. "Right next to St. George."

"Hey, I've been to St. George!" I say excitedly. And then it occurs to me that I'm sounding just like that geek Ed McIff, who's been to St. George, instead of Sergio, who has coolly frolicked with nude princesses in Monaco.

"Yes," snipes Scout. "He stopped there for gas on his way home to Brazil once."

"Brazil." The Beautiful Girl breathes the word like it's

a magic spell. Then she says, "My name is Ellie, by the way. Ellie Fenn. Pleased to meet you both."

"I'm Scout Arrington." Scout sounds all grumpy, like she's being forced against her will to hand over her name to the authorities.

"And I'm . . . Sergio," I remind everyone. Including myself.

"Sergio and Scout. Scout and Sergio," Ellie sings.

Is it just my imagination or does she linger (lovingly!) over the "o" part of my brand-new name?

"You're my first friends in Salt Lake City." Ellie smiles.

"Are my people helping you find everything you need?" Ali asks her. He has mysteriously materialized, casting a shadow over the three of us, not unlike one of those big balloons you see in the Macy's Thanksgiving Day Parade on TV.

Ellie links her arms through mine and Scout's. "Yes, thank you. The service here is excellent." She shoots Ali a wink.

Possibly Ali winks back. It's hard to tell because of the sunglasses. He does, however, give her a wide gleaming smile.

Scout's Take

He stormed through the vicarage door just as she fin-
ished writing the letter. And in spite of the fact that
she was seething with white-hot anger, Clarissa could
not help but notice what a fine figure of a man Lord
Devlin still cut in his riding breeches and mud-
splattered Hessian boots.

I snap shut my book and fling it hard across my
bedroom so that it crashes into the collection of dusty
soccer trophies on my dresser.

As I flop back against my pillow, it occurs to me that
I would have to do VERY serious harm to the person
who discovered that I am sitting in bed in the middle of

the night reading a (yikes!) Regency romance. I would have to blindfold and gag that person, then also interrogate him in a cheap motel room beneath a single naked lightbulb—just to see if he told anybody at school that I actually read books with titles like *Lord Devlin Decides*.

And then I would have to kill him anyway.

I would have to stuff his body in the trunk of my brother Ben's Mustang and dump his body in the Great Salt Lake just to make sure that NO ONE ever found out that Scout Arrington (West High School literary magazine editor and all-state soccer player) is a closet romance reader.

So that's my deep dark secret. Are you shocked?

I started reading Regencies during my Jane Austen phase in the eighth grade. I loved her novels so much that I started looking for similar books to satisfy my cravings between readings of Austen. And I found them.

Sort of.

I mean the stories *are* set in early nineteenth-century England, just like *Pride and Prejudice*. The heroes (who—please see the above quotation—wear Hessian boots) are proud and arrogant like Mr. Darcy. And the heroines (who wear muslin) are spirited and intelligent like Elizabeth Bennet.

But that's pretty much where the similarities end.

Jane Austen was a genius, okay? Her prose is polished and precise, which isn't really something you can say about the prose in *Lord Devlin Decides*.

There's another difference, though. A very BIG difference.

When you read *Pride and Prejudice*, you understand Darcy and Elizabeth are probably lusting after each other in a very polite, well-bred sort of way. Their nostrils may even flare with white-hot emotion, but you don't actually get to hear them pant.

This does NOT happen to be true of Regencies written nowadays, and if you want to know what I'm talking about THEN GO READ ONE FOR YOURSELF AND SHARE MY SECRET SHAME (suggested titles: *The Devil's Dues*, *Reforming the Rake*, *My Lady Lucifer*, and *The Bluestocking's Ball*).

"Scoutie?" My dad, who has obviously heard the clatter of random soccer trophies, calls sleepily down the hall to me. "Are you okay, sweetheart?"

"Sorry I woke you up," I call back. "I'm fine."

And I am fine. I am always fine. Fine, fine, fine, fine. I am Scout Arrington, who is levelheaded and practical and REALLY hardworking and always amazingly, reliably fine.

My only problem at the moment is that Clarissa, the heroine of *Lord Devlin Decides*, reminds me of this girl who came into work tonight, which is why I chucked the stupid book across my bedroom.

Let me tell you about this girl.

She had long, shining yellow hair like Clarissa's

(whereas my long, dark hair is coarse and naturally curly).

She had a softly rounded figure like Clarissa's (whereas I am lean and muscular—and also flat).

She had a charming smile and a pleasing laugh (whereas I have to be honest here and say I have no idea if my smile is charming and if my laugh pleases).

Unlike Clarissa, however, this girl was as dumb as rocks! I know this because she didn't even crack a smile when I made my stupid little joke about Ed (otherwise known as Sergio) speaking "Brazilian" like a native.

Brazilian? Give me a break!

Ed, however, did not seem to notice her lack of an intelligent response. Or maybe he just didn't care. Girls like Ellie seem to have that effect on guys like Ed. On guys period.

Ed.

Ed McIff.

We've been pals since we met as freshmen at West High School. I thought he was funny and creative and nice, in spite of the fact he can be pretty sarcastic at times. Especially about himself. What I like best about him, though, is that he's easy to be with. You can talk to him or not talk to him and it's all good. He makes you feel comfortable in your skin.

So that's the way it's been with us, until last fall when he came to one of my soccer games. We were playing the number-one team in our region, and we surprised everybody by keeping the game tied until I scored a goal just before the final whistle.

Well, Ed just went crazy! He leaped out of the bleachers and raced onto the field where he hugged me hard. Then he lifted me off my feet, swung me around, looked me straight in the eyes, and said with another squeeze that took my breath away, "You are the greatest, Scout Arrington!"

So there we were—our faces inches apart, the October sun shining bright through his light brown hair—and suddenly I realized that I had a huge, big old *thing* for this guy, this friend who was holding me tight against his chest.

Later that night he showed up at my house with a bumper sticker for me: GIRLS RULE!

So. How do I love Ed? Let me count the ways.

1. I love the slow, lazy way he shuffles when he walks and the way he folds his arms across his chest when he listens (okay, technically counts as two ways).
2. I love the way he laughs. His eyes crinkle up— especially the left one—and it is just so CUTE.
3. I love how he comes up with goofy ideas about the movies he wants to make.
4. I love the way he takes something as ordinary as wishing on a star and turns it into something magic—like wishing on the moon.

5. I love how he smells. Is that weird? But I do. He smells like soap.
6. I love the way he smiles.
7. *Especially* the way he smiles.

I keep this information strictly confidential, however. He doesn't like me the same way I like him. Obviously. And it would probably embarrass him to know how I really feel. He might start avoiding me even, which means we would stop talking and then we wouldn't be friends anymore.

I would hate it if we couldn't be friends.

I sigh, roll out of bed, walk across the moonlit floor to pick up my trophies and retrieve my novel, while wondering (in spite of myself) what Ed would look like in Lord Devlin's mud-splattered Hessian boots.

The Letter Ellie Wrote

Dear Mom and Grandma,

Me here! Just a quick note to tell you how truly *great* things are going in Salt Lake City! My new voice teacher (Mr. Ballin) is the best, and I know I'll be making more progress than we could have ever hoped for or even imagined! Thank you so so so *so* much for making this summer possible, Mom. I know how hard you work checking groceries at Lin's. Thinking of you there, always smiling and hardly ever complaining no matter how much your feet hurt, makes me want to do my best.

I promise I will not disappoint you.

I'm practicing hard every day, but I'm having loads of fun, too! Your baby sister, Mary, spoils me rotten, and so does her boyfriend, Rick, who is this truly amazing cook. Last night he made us breadsticks with this yummy dipping sauce, and I ate until I made myself sick. (See? I even have my appetite back.)

I've made a couple friends, too. Their names are Scout (she's a girl, actually) and Sergio! Get this: Sergio is all the way from Brazil, but he speaks English without a trace of an accent. Maybe he's been here since he was a baby. I'll have to ask him. Scout is really nice too, but maybe a little naïve. She told me that Sergio speaks "Brazilian" like a native.

Brazilian. Not Portuguese. See what I mean?

I didn't correct her, because I didn't want to embarrass her. I know how it feels to be embarrassed.

Anyhow! Please please please stop worrying about me. I am so totally happy. That other thing is completely behind me. I promise.

Hugs and kisses from your very own,
Ellie

THE EMAIL ELLIE WANTED TO SEND

SUBJECT: Do I at least?

To J.

You see how I cannot even write out your name because of the pain it causes me?

I was so excited when I received permission to enroll at Dixie State before graduating. High-school classes in the morning! College classes in the afternoon! What could be more perfect?

Who knew that things would end the way they did?

Still, in spite of everything, I miss you. I miss

our talks. I am so lonely here it hurts. Tell me, do you ever think of me? Do I at least trouble your sleep?

With questions unanswered I remain,

Ellie Fenn

From the Lab Book of Quentin Andrews O'Rourke

I, Quentin Andrews O'Rourke, believe in the following things.

I believe in the scientific method.

I believe in empiricism.

I believe that men, in general, can and should choose to be rational creatures.

I believe that I, in particular, am a rational creature.

And I believe that my existence has become excruciatingly, unbearably, mind-numbingly dull.

For many months now, I have been carefully observing the movements of the moon through my telescope in the backyard. Furthermore, I have dutifully and accurately kept track of them in this same journal.

I am nothing if not accurate and dutiful.

Yet, as I look over my notes tonight, I suddenly find myself dissatisfied and restless. My observations are facts devoid of real meaning. Stupid. Pointless. Who cares? What of it? It's not as if I will discover anything new about the moon, staring at it night after night. Lunar research fills volumes. Man has even been to the moon, though there are those who claim the moon landing was only a clever conspiracy, a weakly supported thesis that I unequivocally reject.

But I digress.

What I really want to do is kick over my telescope and toss my notes to the wind!

Except then my father and his newest girlfriend named Ashley (they're watching TV inside) would think I am even more disturbed than they already do.

What is happening to me? WHAT DO I WANT?

I can pinpoint exactly my new restlessness to a night several weeks ago. I was shooting baskets in the light from the street lamps. Dad was working on his car, listening to a radio station that plays the songs he liked when he was growing up in Southern California.

"Hey Quen, this is one of the all-time greats," he shouted at me. "It was the theme song for my junior prom."

Dad is always trying to interest me in popular culture—music, television, movies, novels by Stephen King and John Grisham. As if *any* of these things would make me a better student of the sciences. But I indulge him. I held on to my basketball and sat on the curb near his car, pretending to be interested as I watched a pair of dragonflies flit by.

I, Quentin Andrews O'Rourke, believe that small kindnesses such as these are important.

The song, not surprisingly, was the kind Dad usually favors—emotional and overblown, with violins swelling in the background. "I'm Irish," he always says with a shrug whenever a song makes him cry. "What are you gonna do?"

I myself was neutral about the song. I am often neutral about songs. At the end, however, the singer stopped singing and started reciting a poem—something about a "coldhearted orb."

The moon.

"What did you say the name of this song is?" I asked.

Dad peered out from underneath the car, a surprised smile on his face. "You like this one, Quen?"

I shrugged.

"It's called 'Nights in White Satin' by the Moody Blues," he said nonchalantly. Then he stuck his head back under the car, but not until I heard him say, "Hot damn!"

Later, after Dad was in bed, I got online and Googled the song's lyrics. As I expected they were full of emotional drama. People lamenting. Lonely men crying. Old people wishing. Lovers wrestling.

Things happening at night beneath a high moon.
Things I have chosen to know nothing about.
Why?

Why have I chosen NOT to know? Could this be the subject of an investigation using the scientific method?

1. NAME THE PROBLEM OR QUESTION. (See above.)
2. FORM AN EDUCATED GUESS (that would be my hypothesis) OF THE CAUSE OF THE PROBLEM AND MAKE PREDICTIONS.
3. TEST HYPOTHESIS BY DOING AN EXPERIMENT USING PROPER CONTROLS. (Controls? When it comes to human beings?)
4. ORGANIZE AND INTERPRET DATA. (What do you suggest? Creating a graph? Making a chart? It's not like I'm in the first grade again, tracking how long it takes for lima beans to sprout.)
5. REPORT YOUR RESULTS TO A GROUP. (A group? Who could possibly care? ANSWER: I do.)

I don't know why I do, and so suddenly, too. It's as though I've contracted one of those viruses that hit out of the blue and flatten you.

But there it is. I care.

JUNE 13

ED'S TURN

So. Here it is. The (late) morning after. I'm parked on the couch in front of the television, wondering about a number of things.

First, I'm wondering if I could make Maggie come in here and find the remote so I don't have to get up from the couch.

Second, I'm wondering if that's actually my stomach I spy creeping over the top of my boxers like rising dough. How can this possibly be? I've always been a very skinny guy. When did I start getting a gut? Is this why Scout's been begging me to start working out with her at Body, Inc.?

And I thought she just liked my wonderful company!

Third, I'm wondering how the dragonfly that just flew past my face got into the house.

Fourth, I'm wondering about that girl, Ellie Fenn. Will I see her again? I hope I do.

While I'm mulling these things over, I notice there's one of those talk shows on the television right now where everybody is bragging about the first time they had sex, and I start wondering about something else, namely this: Am I the ONLY living teenage boy in America who hasn't had sex ONCE, let alone THREE or possibly FOUR times? A day? Between classes? In the janitor's closet even?

Trust me on this one. If you watch enough daytime television in the summer, you start thinking thoughts like this on a regular basis.

Just then my mom cruises through with a laundry basket full of socks. "As long as you're sitting there in your boxers rotting your brains out in front of the TV, Ed, you can match these for me."

Great, I think, as I take the basket from her. Now I can be a short, boxer-wearing, weight-gaining, laundry-folding, not-sex-having teenage American guy.

Yes! Just what I always wanted to be!

Mom squints at the TV for a minute and bursts out laughing. Then she looks at me. "Oh stop worrying, Ed," she says breezily. "Believe me, you're not the only teenager in America who isn't having sex. There's plenty of time for that later."

Then she sails out of the room with her invisible crystal ball, leaving me on the couch feeling depressed and really scared of her.

That's when I make two extremely important decisions.

First, I'm going to start working out with Scout so I can turn my stomach into a six-pack. Or possibly even a twelve-pack. Or maybe even a complete crate of soda like the kind Mom buys at Costco.

Second, if Ellie ever comes back to Reel Life, I'm gonna be ready. I'm not gonna blow my chances with her. Do you hear me?

I leave the unfolded socks sitting on the couch, pick up the telephone, and call Scout as Quark's silver-striped cat, Helena, begins to thread herself lovingly through my legs.

Scout's Take

The phone rings and I pick it up. Someone shouts in my ear.

"STOP DOING THAT, HELENA!" This is followed by very loud hissing and meowing. "MAGGIE! GET THIS STUPID CAT OUT OF HERE!"

"Um. Hello?"

"Sorry about that, Scout," Ed bellows. "My neighbor's cat won't leave me alone. She's in love with me."

I laugh. "That's sweet."

"It's not sweet. It's sick! She sneaks into our house and stalks me, even though I am highly allergic to cats."

"Why is she in love with you if she belongs to your neighbor?" I ask, smiling.

Ed heaves a huge mock sigh. "It's like that old comedian guy Woody Allen said when he started dating his own daughter. The heart wants what it wants."

"Technically speaking, Woody Allen wasn't her father," I point out, in the interest of fairness to disgusting and lecherous movie stars. "He wasn't even her stepfather, Ed. He was her mother's lover, which makes him the steplover."

Ed gives a halfhearted, sad little laugh, and I start to wonder if something is wrong.

"What's up?" I ask lightly, although my worry alarm is going off.

"I'm getting a gut, Scout."

Relieved that he's okay, I laugh. "You are not getting a gut. Jeez, Ed, you sound like a girl. Next thing I know you'll be asking me if your pants make your butt look too big."

"Then why do you keep dropping hints about me going to the gym with you?"

This truly takes me by surprise. I pause, wanting to say the words people in Regency romance novels always say.

Because I want to be with you. Always. Anywhere. Even in a gym.

Okay, maybe they don't mention "gyms" in Regency romances. But you get the idea.

"Duh," I say instead. "I just thought it would be fun.

You'd like Body, Inc. Ali works out there too."

"Great!" Ed laughs nervously. "Sign me up then!"

I pause. "Seriously?"

"Yup. If I have to work out, I can't think of anybody I'd rather work out with than you."

My heart skips a beat. Ed wants to be with me! And then he throws a bucket of cold water my way.

"I need you to teach me some Portuguese fast, Scout. I took Spanish in seventh grade. How hard could it be?"

"You're crazy, Ed. Oh, excuse me, *Senhor* Sergio Mendes." I do my all-purpose foreign accent.

"I'm serious about this, Scout," he persists.

"Ed," I say, trying to keep my voice even. "Do you even realize who Sergio Mendes is?"

"Um. Me?"

"No. He is a Brazilian musician who had a group called Brasil '66." Then I tell him about all those old Sergio Mendes albums in my dad's vinyl record collection.

There's a little pause. "No wonder my new name sounded so familiar. I used to be a Latino rock star," Ed observes weakly.

"Why do you want to learn Portuguese anyway, Ed?" I know already, of course, but I want to hear him say it. Call me a masochist, but it's always interesting to watch Ed wrap his nimble brain around things.

"For your information, Scout, Portuguese is a language I happen to admire and respect very much," Ed says. "Sometimes I do nothing all day long except sit around admiring and respecting Portuguese. You can ask my mom, who also admires and respects Portuguese."

He's good. I gotta give the guy credit for that. "Can't help you out, Ed. Too bad, so sad."

He starts to plead. "Come on, Scout. Please. *Please.*"

I don't answer.

"Scout?"

"Tell me the truth. Why do you want to learn Portuguese?"

He lets out a heavy sigh—a real one this time. "Because I'm short," he says simply.

Normally I would laugh at such a goofy answer. For one thing, Ed is not that short. I'm serious. For another, his size doesn't matter. Not to me. Not to anybody. But I can tell he isn't joking with me for once.

"I'm a short guy in boxers who's sick of being from Salt Lake City instead of Brazil," he clarifies.

What could I say after that?

"Well, *sim* means 'yes,'" I say finally. "So *sim*, I guess I can teach you how to count to ten."

"I love to count to ten!" Ed perks up. "Frontwards! Backwards! Sideways!"

I say the numbers and he repeats them after me.

"Now here are the days of the week," I say.

He repeats these, too. Then I teach him how to

greet people and how to respond when they return the greeting.

"Scout," he says when we're through, "I freakin' love you!"

I don't answer. Instead, I just hang up the phone.

ED'S TURN

I check myself out in the rearview mirror of Mom's Geo before I back out of the driveway and head for work.

"*Domingo. Segunda-feira. Terça-feira.*" I try to say the days of the week with "suaveness" as well as "suavity."

Do I look stupid? I put some gel in my hair after washing it this time, and then I slicked it back so that I would exude foreign-ness in general and Brazil-ness in particular. One way or the other, slick hair is definitely a new look for me, the boy who's as American as Velveeta cheese.

"What's up with your hair tonight, Ed?" Mom asked earlier as I floated into the kitchen wearing my newly polished wingtip shoes and grabbed a Capri Sun from the pantry.

"Yeah," chimed in Maggie, who was squirting

strawberry syrup into a glass of milk. "What's up with your hair?"

"I'm trying something new," I told them, bristling. "Can't anybody try something new around this house without mothers and sisters making a freaking federal case out of it?"

An idea for a scene from the yet-to-be-made movie of my life flashed through my mind.

JUDGE:
(pointing at a guy in a Reel Life Movies uniform) Ed McIff! The United States government, whose constitution I have sworn to uphold, chooses to make a federal case out of your stupid hair!

ED:
Please, Your Excellency, I was only trying something new.

JUDGE:
(slamming his gavel) We've sentenced people to life imprisonment with T. Monroe as a cell mate for less than that.

ED:
Your Honor, could you just give me the death penalty instead?

Mom gave me a little hug. "I kind of like the old Ed. What was wrong with him?" She reached out and touched my shining helmet of hair, after which she burst out laughing.

That's my mom for you—the World's Happiest Gal. Gershwin should write a snappy show tune about her. Too bad he's dead.

I adjust the Geo's rearview mirror and touch my hair one more time, praying like crazy that I don't look as stupid as I suspect I do. Then I slip the key in the ignition and turn on the engine.

Nothing.

I try again.

Nada.

Again.

Zip.

I check the lights and swear loudly. Somebody (okay, it was me) left them on, and now the battery is as dead as yesterday's roadkill. Dad, who's out of town, has the other car, and I need to be at work in fifteen minutes.

Ali will be there, watching to see if I make it on time.

I leap out of the car without bothering to shut the door, spring across our front lawn (ruining my newly polished wingtip shoes), and jump over the low boxwood hedge that divides our property from the O'Rourkes'. Whether he wants to or not, Quark is going to haul my sorry carcass to work.

In a flash I'm on the front porch, ringing Quark's doorbell. His dad answers and gives me an easy smile.

"Hey there, Ed," he says.

Sometimes I wonder what Quark's dad must really and truly think about his only kid. Mr. O'Rourke was an All-American football player for Brigham Young University back in the days when Steve Young played there. He's still a big, athletic guy who looks a lot like Quark. That, however, is where the resemblance between father and son ends. Quark is a nerd, a geek, a dork.

Which I am too. Don't get me wrong. But at least I have the decency to recognize the fact. Quark, on the other hand, is completely oblivious to his own NQ (nerd quotient).

"Is Quark here?"

"He's out back, messing around with that telescope of his," Mr. O'Rourke says with the tone of bewildered affection he always uses when he talks about Quark. He pushes open the door and invites me to walk through the house to the backyard.

Quark is looking through his telescope, even though it's still light outside.

I cut to the chase. "My car won't start. I gotta be there in fifteen minutes, or I'll get fired, Ali said. Can you take me?"

Quark doesn't answer immediately because answering immediately would show that you have some actual social skills.

Which Quark does not.

I don't mean to be unkind when I tell you this. I like Quark a lot. He and Scout are my best friends. It's just that Quark doesn't pay attention to all the little unwritten social rules that the rest of us do.

"Quark?"

He stands up to his full height. Watching Quark stand up is like watching the *Niña*, the *Pinta*, and the *Santa María* unfurl their mainsails. He's that tall.

"I heard you," he says. "Let's go."

I keep touching my hair on the way to work, still wondering if I look stupid. Although I am fixated on my hair at the moment, I do notice that Quark is performing what sounds like the drum solo from "Wipe Out" with his fingers on the steering wheel.

Okay. Guys all over America do this on a daily basis when they drive. It's written in the Handbook for American Guys that they must do drum solos on steering wheels whenever they get the chance.

But not Quark. Quark doesn't listen to music with drum solos. He listens to classical.

"What's up with you?" I ask.

"Nothing," he says.

I shrug and then throw him a question straight out of left field. "What do you know about Brazil these days, Quark?"

"I did a report on Brazil in the fifth grade," Quark

says. "That was a few years ago, of course, but I suspect much of the information still pertains."

"Dude! Lucky for me," I say.

"Brazil," begins Quark, "is a beautiful country full of rain forests that shelter a rich and varied bird population. . . ."

When we pull into the Reel Life parking lot, Quark (the Brazilian bird expert) surprises me some more.

"I think I'll come inside and—you know—rent a DVD," he says.

First the drum solo. Now this.

I'm pretty sure the last time Quark saw a movie was when he and I were kids and my mom took us to see *The Little Mermaid* at the old Villa Theater with her and Maggie. The experience put Quark off of movies for good. I think it also made him a little afraid of my mother. He gets that deer-in-the-headlights look whenever she says hello to him, like he's terrified she's going to stuff him in the trunk of her car and force him to watch *The Little Mermaid* again.

"A DVD, Quark?" I whistle as I crawl out of the car. "Wow!"

"So," he says, slamming his door shut, "what do you recommend?"

What would *you* recommend to someone like Quark if you were me?

"Well, we have some very good documentaries," I say.

Quark actually lets rip with a snort of contempt, which surprises me as much as the drum solo and the sudden interest in finding a good DVD. Quark is not a snorter by nature. One of the things I like best about Quark, in fact, is that he never snorts when I say something stupid. Which is often. Which is why I appreciate the way Quark usually lets my comments wash over him like waves on a beach.

"Are you okay?" I ask as we walk through the parking lot together. "You're pretty much not acting like yourself tonight."

"I'm fine," he says. "I just want to watch something else besides a documentary now and then. I *am* a human being, you know, Ed."

I clutch my head as I stagger through the front door and bellow loudly (like the Elephant Man), "I'm a human being! I'm not an animal! I'M A HUMAN BEING!"

Startled, several Reel Life customers look up from the racks and stare. Quark blinks in confusion. T. Monroe purses his thin lips and shoots me a prissy look. Scout busts loose with a hearty laugh.

"Six o'clock on the money," Ali says. "You're getting better, McIff."

"Thanks," I say quickly. Also respectfully. Without making eye contact.

I glance up at Quark to see if he enjoyed my impromptu Elephant Man monologue, but he isn't paying attention to me. He's way too busy looking at Scout, who's working with T. Monroe behind the front counter.

"Do you think it's a sin to accidentally swallow a fingernail you've bitten off when you're supposed to be fasting?" T. Monroe is asking Scout.

"T. Monroe is a Jesus freak," I explain under my breath to Quark.

"Do not disrespect my man T. Monroe," says Ali, suddenly materializing behind me and Quark. "He knows exactly who he is, and he keeps the rest of us honest."

I mumble a hasty apology to Ali, while Quark keeps staring at Scout.

Actually, "staring" is putting it way, way, way too mildly. He is "gazing" at Scout as though she were the moon. Any minute now his eyeballs are gonna pop out and roll around the carpet.

"Scout," I say, "you remember my neighbor, Quark."

Scout smiles. "Sure. How are you, Quark?"

Quark stands rooted to the spot like the tallest tree in a forest of very tall trees. His mouth is slightly ajar, like the door of a large American car.

"Did you come to hang out with me and Ed, or can I actually help you find something?"

Quark talks like he's in a dream. "Yes. Thank you very much. Thank you very, very, very much, Scout." He blushes—*blushes!*—when he says her name.

Scout gives a light shrug and a friendly smile. "No *problemo*. What kind of movies do you like?"

"Don't listen to him," I volunteer. "He probably likes films with subtitles."

Quark is the kind of guy who wouldn't mind reading to pass the time at a movie.

"I didn't ask you what Quark likes, Ed." Scout frowns at me. "I asked Quark." She bathes him in her best Employee-of-the-Month smile.

"I enjoy the so-called screwball comedies from the 1930s." Quark says this in the exact same way a very bad actor says lines he has memorized (barely) for a very bad scene in a very bad movie. Naturally I do not believe him for a second. Screwball comedies? Please. This is clearly a term he's recently picked up while listening to NPR or surfing the 'net.

"Quark," I say sternly. "Am I going to have to take you into the men's room and give you a swirlie? Don't stand there telling Scout you like screwball comedies. You're embarrassing yourself."

"But I *love* screwball comedies," Scout says, her entire countenance lighting up like a scoreboard at a soccer game. "*Topper, Bringing Up Baby, The Awful Truth.* Those are such incredibly great movies!"

"Yes," says Quark the Liar. "I agree."

"Which is your favorite?" Scout leans across the counter and glows at him.

"It would be difficult for me to say," Quark muses.

"No kidding," I say.

"I know what you mean." Scout nods at Quark while ignoring me completely. "Although I pretty much love any film with Cary Grant in it."

"Yes," says Quark the Double Liar. "I agree. Cary Grant is 'the man.'"

I groan. Do my ears deceive me?

"Hey!" Scout says, ignoring me still. "Maybe we could have a screwball comedy film festival. We could sit together in my basement, eating popcorn—the real kind, drenched in butter, not microwaved—and watch old movies for hours and hours."

Quark's jaw unhinges again.

As for me, I just stand there in my frilly white Reel Life shirt, gaping at my two best friends. To tell you the truth, I feel like I'm watching an updated version of *Invasion of the Body Snatchers* set in Salt Lake City.

FIRST ALIEN:
Do you see the male earthling called Quark and the female earthling called Scout?
SECOND ALIEN:
Yes, O High Commander. I see them.

FIRST ALIEN:

Let's go snatch their bodies and turn them into sorry movie geeks who enjoy the so-called screwball comedies from the 1930s.

SECOND ALIEN:

I hear and obey.

One of the really great things about Scout is that she is an Honorary Guy. She likes guy stuff, including guy movies. Whenever Ali and Scout and I have to close on a Saturday night, we'll put on a Jackie Chan flick, and Scout almost dies on the spot from pure cinematic happiness. She loves action movies. NOT screwball comedies from the 1930s.

Trust me on this one. I, Ed McIff, know Scout Arrington inside and out.

Quark hangs around for a good thirty minutes, shambling after Scout. If I didn't know Quark as well as I do, I'd almost say he has a thing for her.

Quark? Interested? Oh ha, frickety ha! Please don't make me laugh!

Quark finally makes a move to leave about the time a group of Trekkies dressed as their favorite characters walks through the door. Although Trekkies drive me crazy, I have to admit that the guy who's dressed as Worf looks pretty sharp. Maybe I could go as Worf to Ali's costume ball and earn a little respect for a change.

"Dude," I say to Worf. "Where'd you get your outfit?"

He answers me in a guttural language that sounds like the Orcs in *Lord of the Rings*.

"He's speaking Klingon," Captain Picard informs me. He turns to Worf and issues a crisp mandate. "As your commanding officer, I advise that you speak to him in his own language."

Quark looks intrigued by this unexpected exchange between Reel Life customers, while Scout works hard to swallow a smile.

"That would be English," I tell Worf.

"And also Brazilian," Scout adds. "He's bilingual."

"As am I," Worf says. "I started teaching myself Klingon when I was in the fifth grade."

"Impressive," says Quark. Unlike me and Scout, he's serious.

"Everything you need to know about the language is online if you're interested," says Worf. He turns to me. "You can rent an outfit at the Costume Shoppe on Thirty-third South, by the way."

"Great," I say. "Thanks."

"Gay'be'!" he says—whatever that means.

As Worf and his posse walk away, Quark reluctantly picks up his pile of fifteen DVDs, and smiles one last time at Scout as he walks toward the exit.

"Yes, well," he says, still smiling over his shoulder

at Scout. "Thanks again."

"My pleasure." Scout beams back.

BAM! Quark misses the door by a mile and plows straight into the plate-glass window. He hits it with such force that the DVDs fly out of his arms like a flock of birds.

I burst out laughing. Meanwhile, Quark stoops over to pick up the DVDs and manages to bang his head into the window again.

Scout glowers at me and then scrambles to Quark's side to lend a helping hand. "Are you okay?" she asks.

"Jeez, Quark," I say. "Since when did you start using your melon as a wrecking ball?"

Quark chooses to ignore this.

"Thank you so much," he says instead to Scout, as she piles DVDs into his waiting arms. "May I also compliment you on having such beautiful windows. They are the cleanest, most beautiful windows I have ever seen in a business establishment. I mean that sincerely."

As this point, I am nearly DEAD with sympathetic embarrassment for Quark.

What's sympathetic embarrassment? you ask. You know how some husbands start suffering from morning sickness when their wives get pregnant? That's called sympathetic pregnancy. Well, sympathetic embarrassment is when you start feeling the extreme social pain someone else SHOULD be feeling for himself because he's done something stupid. Such as crashing into a plate-glass window twice, for example.

"McIff!" Ali barks.

I am, as always, all ears when it comes to Ali.

"Help your boy out to his car."

I sketch Ali a quick salute and do as I am bid.

"What is with you?" I ask Quark as we walk back through the parking lot.

His mouth is pressed into a thin line. He doesn't answer.

"You look like you just swallowed your lips, Quark," I point out.

He still doesn't say anything—just unlocks his trunk and dumps all those great screwball comedies (from the 1930s) inside.

"Hey! Careful with the merchandise there, pal!" I warn.

Quark slams the trunk shut.

"Screwball comedies?" I say. "What was that all about? If I didn't know you better, I'd say you had a thing for Scout! Ha! Ha! You and Scout!"

Quark bends over to get into my face. His cheeks are blotchy and his nose is red, besides which it is starting to swell.

"Shut up, Ed," he says. "Just shut the bloody hell up. And by the way, you can find your own damn ride home!"

Shaken, I walk back into Reel Life.

"Is Quark okay?" Scout asks.

"I honestly don't know," I say.

Scout chews on her lower lip thoughtfully as she stares out at the parking lot. "He's a good guy, isn't he."

"He is," I say, "although I'm sorry if he bugged you, Scout. Neither Quark nor I get out much, which makes us both act like dorks when we're in public."

"Relax." Scout laughs. "He didn't annoy me at all. In fact, I enjoyed talking to him."

I breathe a sigh of relief.

Here's the thing. Quark *is* strange. There's just no getting around that fact. And I *do* give him a pretty bad time because that's the only way I have of keeping his Mr. Wizard weirdness from making me crazy. Still, underneath the goofiness, Quark is a truly decent person. One of the best. And I would have felt really, really bad if Scout, without knowing what a good guy he is, had turned Quark into a joke behind his back.

I'm just getting ready to go on my ten p.m. break when Ellie walks through the door, looking as fresh as flowers.

Well, maybe not flowers. That's the kind of clichéd and stale comparison that English teachers like to humiliate their students for making. But Ellie does look fresh. And beautiful, too, with straight and shining hair falling long down her back.

Suddenly I can see the two of us in a movie together.

*Ellie walks into the video store where I'm working.
Wearing a white hat with a very large brim, she turns
so that I (the world-weary and cynical owner of the
store) catch my breath as I see her lovely face.*

ME:
(doing a voice-over) Of all the cheap, two-bit video
joints, she has to walk into mine.

Quickly I touch my hair. I'm sure you'll be relieved to
learn it's still there.

"*Alô,* Ellie," I say with a big Brazilian smile. "*Como vai?*"

I can't believe it. Her blue eyes actually a) brighten
and b) widen with delighted surprise. For the record,
this is the sort of reaction that Ed never gets.

"Sergio! I was hoping you'd be here tonight!" Ellie
glances around until she spies Scout. "Hey, Scout!" Ellie
calls over the heads of customers while waving enthusi-
astically.

Scout, who looks like she's just swallowed a large dish
of stewed prunes, returns Ellie's greeting with the sort of
small, stiff wave favored by members of the British royal
family.

"Isn't she the best?" Ellie asks, turning her blue gaze
on me again.

"The best," I agree. Then dropping my voice, I add,
"And so are you."

Ellie (who turns an attractive shade of shell pink) smiles shyly at me.

Okay. I can feel it. I am totally losing my head.

"Say something in Portuguese for me, Sergio," Ellie says.

I start counting, rolling my r's like crazy so that they sound just like big, wild waves crashing over movie stars making out on the beach.

Ellie's smile broadens. "What are you saying, Sergio? It sounds so . . . romantic. Is it?"

"Yes," I say. "It's a love poem about—"

"Numbers," says Scout as she walks up behind me. "Brazilians love doing math so much, they write romantic poems about numbers. Isn't that right, *Sergio*?"

I feel like a balloon after the air has just whooshed out of it. *"Sim,"* I say. "That is very true. My people love math. We cannot help ourselves."

Ellie looks totally confused but manages to rally. "Oh. That's really interesting. I love learning interesting things about other cultures. Don't you, Scout?"

"Sim," says Scout, glaring at me.

Just then Ali whistles for me like he's Captain von Trapp and I am one of his sissy sons in a sailor suit.

"Sir!"

"Go on break," he orders. "Scout, baby, I need you over here."

"Gotta run," says Scout. *"Adeus."*

"Do you want to go on break with me?" I ask Ellie.

Full of smiles for Sergio, she nods.

I buy Ellie and me some Snelgrove's ice cream at Squirrel Brothers next door. She orders burnt almond fudge in a waffle cone, which happens to be Scout's favorite too. Together we sit at a café table outside and stare at the sky.

"There sure are a lot of stars out tonight," she says. "I've noticed that you don't usually see this many here because of all the city lights. At home there are stars to spare."

Did I just hear a touch of loneliness in her voice?

"Do you miss home?" I ask.

She looks at me and smiles brightly. "No."

I look at her, not sure if she's telling me the truth.

"What about you, Sergio?" Ellie asks. "Do you miss Brazil?"

I squirm a little. "I don't remember that much about it, to tell you the truth."

She looks disappointed, and the very last thing I want to do right now is disappoint this girl.

"I do, however, remember the rain forests that shelter a rich and varied bird population," I say.

"Oh, I love birds! I love the music they make!" Ellie says. "Tell me about the birds, Sergio."

I look at the sky above. "See all those stars up there?

Well, in Brazil there are as many birds as there are stars."

"Birds like stars," Ellie breathes.

"Yes, only they're all different colors. Green and pink and peacock blue with tail feathers that stream out behind them so that they look like—" I draw a blank.

"Like *shooting* stars." Ellie finishes my simile for me.

"Exactly! Like shooting stars."

"Imagine," she whispers. "Birds like singing shooting stars."

And here's the thing. I really can imagine it just the way I said it—bright jungle skies filled with birds swirling around and around like shooting stars, green and pink and peacock blue.

Ellie and I look straight into each other's eyes. We don't say words.

We don't need to.

The Letter Ellie Wrote

Dear Mom and Grandma,

I saw my friends Scout and Sergio again tonight, and we had a great time! Sergio told me some very interesting things about Brazil. Did you know the skies are constantly filled with all kinds of birds there? Meanwhile, Mary keeps buying me sinful chocolates from a place called Cummings on Seventh East—I like the Rum Victoria the best—and Rick keeps fixing these amazing dinners—clam linguine and Caesar salad last night.

How could I not be happy here? Stop worrying about me. That's an order!

Tell grumpy Mr. Hurst at the grocery store that I actually miss him. Say hello to Mrs. Hafen and yummy baby Isaac next door. Promise Boots I'll bring him home a can of gourmet cat food. But only if he stops picking on the dogs.

Love always,

Ellie

P.S. What's blooming in the garden right now, Gran?

THE EMAIL ELLIE WANTED TO SEND

SUBJECT: Intruding . . .

To J.

And still I miss you.

I try not to. Instead I try to think of other things I love—burnt red hills, the dark-haired and brown-skinned baby next door, Gran's garden full of lilacs and blue iris in the spring and star jasmine and honeysuckle in the summer, the lyrics to *La Wally*, which I am learning now.

I try to memorize the lyrics when I feel the memory of you walking toward me. I try to hear in my

head how I'll shape the sounds.
But still you intrude.
You intrude.

Ellie Fenn

Scout's Take

He was counting. *Counting*, if you please. With a *stupid* grin on his face. Pretending that he was doing something very sophisticated, very romantic—such as reciting poetry.

Not just poetry. Love-with-a-capital-L poetry.

So here's my question. Will any boy ever be remotely tempted to recite love poetry to me? Or will I always be treated just like "one of the guys"?

A girl like Ellie, on the other hand, with her blond hair and velvety skin, inspires love poetry even when it isn't actually love poetry. Even when it's just ordinal numbers in Portuguese recited over the checkout desk at a movie rental store.

Things are always different for girls like Ellie. Girls

like Ellie never sit in their rooms late at night reading romances on the sly. They get to live romances.

I want to hate Ellie. Really and truly I do. With all my heart. In fact, I want to make hating Ellie my latest hobby. That way whenever I have to list my hobbies on a resume, I can put "creative writing, playing soccer, watching screwball comedies, and hating Ellie" in the space provided below. I can raise hating Ellie to the level of high art. I can be the founder and president of the Ellie Un-Fan Club populated by average-looking girls like me. We can get together on a monthly basis and think of mean things to do to Ellie's shining, perfect hair when she's asleep.

Only I don't hate Ellie. Not at all.

How could I? I'm on her radar screen even though she's gorgeous and I'm not. She walks into Reel Life and immediately acknowledges me even before she says hello to Ed/Sergio. The truth is she's nice.

Besides, I don't think it's in my nature to hate people, even when they deserve to be hated. I can even give you a specific example.

Last year my grandfather, who is a very prominent bone doctor and former church leader here in Salt Lake City, got his twenty-three-year-old nurse pregnant.

Oh! Oops!

Being an honorable man, he thought it only right to divorce his wife of forty years (my grandmother) and marry the nurse (my stepgrandmother—she's the one with dollar signs in her eyes) so that the poor baby (my half aunt) would have a first name (Samantha) and a last name (Arrington).

Of course everybody in the entire extended family has stopped speaking to him. Hating Grandpa has become a family obligation. We've begun having family reunions just so we can all get together and play horseshoes and volleyball while hating our grandfather the Adulterer.

And I do hate what he did. I hate it with all my heart. How can a supposedly smart person give up so much for sex, and then pretend to himself and everyone else afterward that it wasn't really about the sex?

Only as it turns out I don't hate him.

I can't forget how he took me fishing on the Provo River when I was a little girl and how he taught me stupid songs about burping. I can't forget how he played card games with me when all the other grown-ups were too busy talking and how HE was the one who could always get splinters out of my bare feet and gum out of my hair without hurting me.

And I won't forget how he still comes to my soccer games, even though he has to sit in different bleachers from the rest of my family.

Love.

Who needs it?

ED'S TURN

Birds like stars.

I'm just lying here in bed, thinking about how amazing it is that I actually said something like that to a beautiful girl without sounding pathetic. But then I guess Ed didn't really say those words. Sergio did.

Man, I just love being Sergio.

I look out the window by my bed one more time before rolling over to go to sleep. Birds like stars. Even the moon reminds me of a bird tonight. A fat white swan, paddling slowly across a murky lake of sky, silent and full of secrets.

From the Lab Book of Quentin Andrews O'Rourke

When I am being honest with myself I can, of course, account for my enduring fascination with the moon.

My mother used to read *Goodnight Moon* to me when I was little. I used to love to hear her low voice as I stared out my bedroom window.

> *In the great green room*
> *There was a telephone*
> *And a red balloon*
> *And a picture of—*
> *The cow jumping over the moon . . .*

It's such a comforting book. Just a bunny and his mother in a roomful of familiar things. No surprises. Just things the way the bunny expects them to be. Just things the way they're supposed to be.

It wasn't long before I started looking for the moon in the night sky myself. Of course, I noticed right away that the moon doesn't stay the same—not like the pictures in my book.

"Look," I said to my mother one night when the moon was in an early phase. I was probably three or four years old, and I was truly alarmed. "Something happened to the moon. It's broken!"

My mother laughed. "What a funny little boy you are!" Then she took my hand. "You remind me of myself, Quentin. Full of imagination. Full of mystery. Unknowable. Just like the moon."

Only I learned that the moon, in fact, is not full of mystery.

The moon is as predictable as it is knowable. . . .

Or so I thought.

I met Ed's friend Scout again. I've met her before, of course, but I wasn't paying attention. Today, however, I looked straight into her eyes and saw that they are dark brown and shot with gold.

She makes me want to get online and Google "screwball comedies."

She makes me want to take a chance.

Which is why I, Quentin Andrews O'Rourke, have decided to surrender. I hereby surrender myself to the MYSTERIES of the moon.

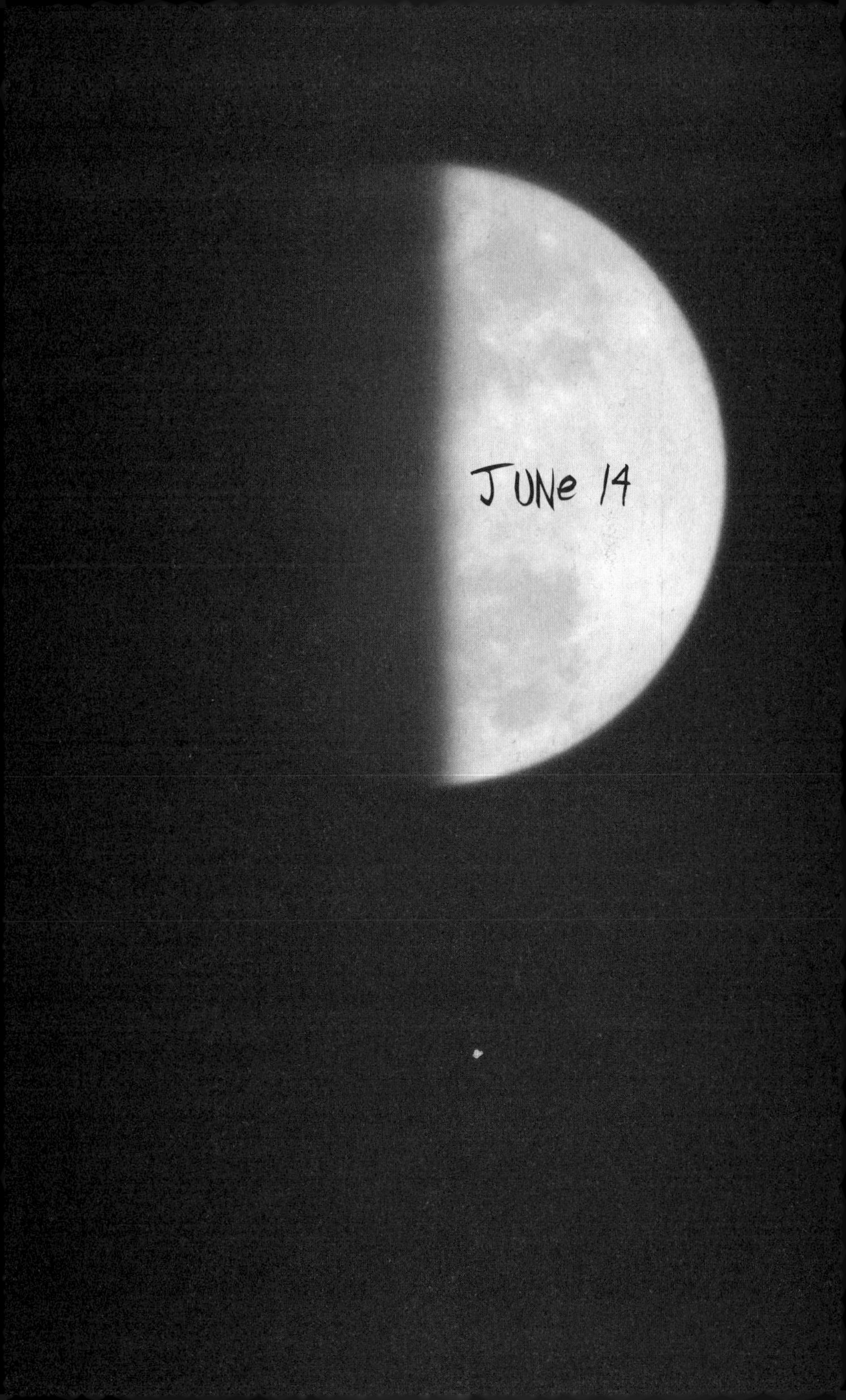
JUNE 14

ED'S TURN

Tonight I am working with Ali (who makes me nervous) and T. Monroe (who makes me crazy). Scout has the evening off, and I really miss her. In fact, I want to call her up on the telephone and say, "Scout! Come to work RIGHT NOW so that life will be good again!"

T. Monroe is rewinding one of the few videos we still carry, and I decide to make the time go a little faster by engaging in some friendly employee small talk.

"So what are you wearing to Ali's party, T. Monroe?"

I am pretty worried about this entire issue, actually. I can just see me and my lovely date, Quark, two boring dorks in totally uninspired costumes surrounded by fascinating guests wearing wild and exotic creations made from the feathers of parrots.

Or something along those lines.

Without looking up from his stack of videos, T. Monroe starts quoting scripture at me. "'And why take ye thought for raiment? Consider the lilies of the field, how they grow; they toil not, neither do they spin. And yet I say unto you, That even Solomon in all his glory was not arrayed like one of these.'"

"Thank you very much, T. Monroe," I say. "I'll be sure to keep that in mind."

I turn my back on him and make a mental note to myself to line up a Worf costume by next Thursday. Also, I've gone online a few times to find a few choice Klingon curses. Stuff like "Your mother has a smooth face," which apparently is the ultimate Klingon dis.

Then I think of Ellie's smooth face and wonder whether or not she'll come by tonight.

I hope she does because, hoo-boy, did I ever do my homework THIS TIME.

Here's what I did. When I took Maggie shopping at Trolley Square earlier today, I checked out the Brazilian restaurant there called the Rodizio Grill. I immediately trotted inside and asked the hostess (dressed up like a girl gaucho) if I could look at a menu. Then (because I learned how to be prepared that one time I went to Boy Scouts) I pulled a pencil and a crumpled-up overdue parking ticket out of my back pocket and jotted down the names of a few authentic dishes.

If Ellie comes into Reel Life tonight, I plan to tell her about the rich and varied dishes served in my beloved homeland.

Ellie walks through the door like Cinderella just before the clock strikes midnight.

Actually, it was only about ten, but you know how I am—unable to resist the dramatic touch.

"Hi, Sergio," she says with a shimmering smile.

"*Alô*, Ellie," I say, full of Brazilian swagger.

"How are things?"

"Things are going very well now that you are here." I look at her with eyes full of meaning, and she laughs agreeably because I am so charming. I am charming Sergio.

A little silence grows between us. If I were still Ed, I would start to worry perhaps. I would think that we had run out of things to say. I would start to sweat, and probably not a manly sweat, either.

But now that I am Sergio, I know there is plenty left to be said. And unsaid. Because I am Sergio, I also realize Ellie is flirting with me by the way she is playing with her beautiful hair. Ed would not have understood this.

She smiles at me again, and then puts her elbows on the counter and rests her heart-shaped face in her hands. "Tell me some more about Brazil, Sergio. Please."

I lean toward her. "Let me tell you about the wonderful food my grandmother used to fix for us."

Elli's face brightens even more. "I'd love to hear all about it."

"Well," I say, "let me start you off with a few verbal appetizers."

And I tell her about *pãozinho* and *pão de queijo*, *polenta*, and *banana frita*.

"*Banana frita?*" says Ellie. "What's that?"

"Glazed banana," I say slickly, even though it could be an unglazed banana for all I know. "With lots of cinnamon." The lies just come pouring out of me.

"Cinnamon?" Ellie darts a tiny pink tongue over her lips, tasting the imaginary cinnamon there.

And I practically stop breathing.

The Letter Ellie Wrote

Dear Mom and Grandma,

How would you like me to cook Brazilian for you when I come home? I'm going to have Rick teach me how! Here's the amazing thing. It turns out Rick was on a mission to Brazil the same time grumpy Mr. Hurst's grandson (the one who dyed his hair green when we were in high school) was there. Mormondom is such an amazingly small world! Six degrees of separation and all that!

Anyway, I think it will be fun to have *Senhor* Rick give me cooking lessons. He's so wonderful. I think Mary has finally found someone who's good enough for her.

Hugs!
Ellie

THE EMAIL ELLIE WANTED TO SEND

SUBJECT: Chanceless

To J.

How did I love thee? Let me count the ways.

First, I loved how smart you are.

Second, I loved all the things you know about books and paintings and especially music, and I loved how you shared those things with me.

Third, I loved the way you told me about the places you've been because I want to see the world—all of it—for myself, although I worry that I will always be just Ellie from Santa Clara who never has that chance.

Fourth, and oh yes, I loved the way you look.
But not until I loved the inside of you first.
I never shared this list with you because I would
have felt silly.
And now I'll never have the chance.

Chanceless in Salt Lake City,

Ellie Fenn

JUNe 15

Scout's Take

The phone rings and I pick it up. "Hello?"

"Scout! Thank goodness you're home!" It's my mom, calling from work and sounding desperate. "I forgot to pick up Benny's new contacts at the eye doctor on my lunch break. Can you get them for me, then FedEx a package off to Brazil this afternoon?"

I groan a little. I hate it when I have to run errands for Mom.

"Please, Scout? Benny's sick of bumping into banana trees because he can't see."

I laugh in spite of myself.

"The doctor's office is by the Foothill Branch Library, Scout," Mom wheedles. "You know where that is, don't you?"

Of course I do. It's not far from Ed's house.

Mom still wheedles. "You might find something new there you'd like to read"—she lowers her voice here—". . . if you know what I mean."

I know EXACTLY what she means.

"Fine," I huff, totally hating myself for being addicted to love of the Regency romance variety. "I'll take care of it."

Mom laughs and says good-bye.

I hang up (hard) and stare at the phone, thinking how much I hate it when mothers exploit the weaknesses of their children to accomplish their own ends. In fact, I think it's completely evil.

Don't you?

ED'S TURN

"Jeez, Quark! You scared the snot out of that poor old lady standing on the corner there!"

I look in the rearview mirror of Quark's car, just in time to catch sight of the aforementioned elderly person jumping up and down the sidewalk, giving us the finger.

It always gives me a start when senior citizens flip me off.

Quark takes another corner, this time (I swear) on two wheels. It's like we're in that old Disney flick *The Love Bug.*

Cut to a scene of an insane Herbie the Love Bug racing out of control through the tree-lined streets of Salt

Lake City's east bench. Inside the car, Ed and Quark (both of them wearing special racing gear) hang on for dear life as they wonder what has gotten into their old reliable friend, Herbie.

QUARK:

Exactly how many little old ladies has Herbie taken out this afternoon, Ed?

ED:

I'm not sure, Quark, but watch out because here comes another one now!

LITTLE OLD LADY:

(tossing her sack of groceries into the air as Herbie comes barreling down on her) AAARGH!

"Dude! Quark!" I gargle. "I want to arrive alive!"

He totally ignores me as he continues to blast down Foothill Boulevard. Roger Ramjet (otherwise known as my buddy Quark) makes one last terrifying turn, and then comes to a screeching halt in front of the Foothill Branch Library. Rubber-legged, I crawl out of the car like an astronaut who's just been taken for a little joyride in *Apollo 13*.

"Remind me to take the bus next time, okay?" I shout after Quark, who is already loping toward the library's entrance like a giraffe traveling at high speed across the grasslands of Africa.

My sarcasm, in case you're interested, is completely lost on him.

I know. I'm being a jerk, especially since Quark has been nice enough to bring me here so I can check out some guide books on my homeland, Brazil.

"Hello, Quark. Hey there, Ed." Our good friend Dody the librarian greets us as I trail Quark inside.

Quark doesn't respond but heads straight for the stacks, his good-looking face screwed up in thought.

"What's up with him?" Dody asks, glancing back over her shoulder at Quark. "Is it just my imagination, or is our lovable genius even more preoccupied than usual?"

I shrug and remember the way he nearly walked through plate-glass windows at Reel Life the other night. "He's been acting pretty strange lately. Stranger than usual that is," I add for clarification purposes.

Dody observes Quark's movements through her bifocals. "What's he doing in the poetry section?"

I gape. "Poetry? Quark hates poetry! Quark thinks poetry sucks."

Dody keeps watching Quark as he accidentally knocks one book after another off the shelves.

"Have you ever read the book *The Man Who Mistook His Wife for a Hat*?" she asks.

"No," I say. "Nobody told me I was supposed to."

Dody ignores my wisecrack. "It's about what happens to people who get brain disorders." She pauses. "Has

Quark had a head injury lately?"

"I don't know," I say slowly, wondering if this could account for Quark's recent behavior. "He did walk into a window the other day."

Quark apparently discovers what he's been looking for, because he snatches a thick book from the stacks and sits down at a nearby table. I say good-bye to Dody and join him.

"Don't you think she has beautiful eyes?" Quark asks.

"Dody?" It's very true that our friend Dody is one fine-looking librarian. But still. She's like about sixty years old. I'm surprised Quark would notice her eyes. Or anybody else's eyes.

Quark stares at me, then blinks in pure surprise. "I'm not referring to Dody, Ed. I'm talking about Scout."

"Scout?" I squeak.

"Scout Arrington," Quark repeats, looking at me in disgust because I am so very dense. "Your coworker."

I reach across the table and slap Quark upside the head. "I know who Scout is!"

Quark blinks, then carries on. "I've been trying to compare her eyes to something that sparkles, which is why I thought of comparing them to geodes, as in 'her eyes sparkle like geodes.'"

Geodes? The last time I thought of geodes was in the third grade during our rocks and minerals unit.

"I'm not sure the image works, however. The only

word I can find that rhymes with 'geode' is 'freeload.'"

Quark shakes his head. "I'm looking for a new direction."

He flips open the fat book, an anthology entitled *Great Love Poems of the Western World*. Meanwhile, I cannot speak. All I can manage is a weak gurgle.

Quark looks up and blinks.

At last I find my tongue. "Are you okay, Quark?"

He blinks again. Quark is one of those habitual blinkers.

I check to see if his pupils are unnaturally dilated. "Just how hard did you hit your head at Reel Life, anyway?"

Quark snorts at me for the second time in a week. "Don't be a moron, Ed."

I grab *Great Love Poems of the Western World* and smack him with it.

"Hello! I am not the moron here, Quark. I am not the one making up poems about geodes!" I glare at him.

Suddenly, Quark bursts out laughing, which causes me to fire out of my seat like a bottle rocket on the Fourth of July.

Trust me on this one. A burst of sudden laughter from Quentin Andrews O'Rourke is one of life's more unnerving experiences. Fault lines shift when Quark laughs. Mountain ranges crumble. Tidal waves come crashing to the shore. Planets are blasted from their orbits and new black holes appear unexpectedly in the universe. This is because Quark laughs louder than any other human being in the history of the world.

Several people tell Quark to shush, including a vagrant who's trying to sleep while pretending to read the morning paper.

Quark stops laughing but his smile remains, and if you were a stranger who had just walked into the library, you would look at him and wonder who this incredibly handsome movie star was, just slumming the morning away in a city library with some nerdy little geek like me.

Quark and Dork. That would be us.

Suddenly I feel so depressed, I want to start smacking myself with *Great Love Poems of the Western World*.

And still Quark keeps on smiling. He just keeps on putting out miles and miles of smiles and smiles.

"What are you so damn happy about?" I snap.

"I'm in love," he says simply.

ED'S TURN (AGAIN!)

Quark? In love?

HOW CAN THIS BE POSSIBLE?

He's never been interested in someone before, and I can't say I blame him.

See, Quark and his father live by themselves because Quark's mother, who is UBER Lovely and Talented, left home when Quark and I were in the third grade. Why? She wanted to be an actress.

Oh. Excuse me. *Actor.*

Quark's mom really lays into people when they make that mistake.

Anyway, she was already an actor here, appearing in local television commercials and theatrical productions in which she was always the star. Like if someone did *The Music Man*, for example, she was always the hot singing librarian.

The truth is Quark's mom has an amazingly sexy voice. I know this is kind of a sick thing to say about your best friend's mother. But it's true. Even when I was a little boy I used to like to hear her say stuff, even if it was just "Quentin! Don't wear your socks outside unless you have shoes on."

Quark's mom wasn't all that happy in Salt Lake City, though. She wanted to be a professional actor, so she packed her bags and headed for New York City, where she (SURPRISE!) ended up getting a part in a well-known soap opera. I guess this is one of those real-life fairy tales. Quark's mom is Cinderella, and she gets to live happily ever after on the Upper West Side of Manhattan with her fluffy shih tzu named Prince Charming.

You might even know who she is, too, only I can't tell you her stage name because I have been forbidden to speak it by my own mother.

My mom hates Quark's mom, which is amazing given the fact that my mother is the original Gal with the Sunny Disposition. She laughs! She sings! She tells jokes! She does imitations! She tap-dances on the kitchen floor to liven things up, and she can still do a split, just like a Rockette! She loves everybody, even crazy Tony down the street, who wears ski goggles in the summer and thinks aliens are trying to poison him and his one-eyed cat.

She liked Quark's mom once upon a time too. They used to jog together every morning. But then Quark's mom split.

"Why did Quark's mom go away?" I asked when it had finally become clear to me that Mrs. O'Rourke wasn't coming back home to take care of Quark. Mom and I were in the kitchen listening to the radio together. I was doing homework at the counter and Mom was peeling potatoes.

She put down her knife and looked at me hard. "She's in love, my sweet honey bunny, and when some people are in love, they think they're entitled to do whatever they want to do, no matter who they hurt."

I scrunched up my face. "Who's Mrs. O'Rourke in love with?" I was still young enough to believe all parents were in love with each other.

"Herself," Mom said with a tiny bitter smile. "She's in love with herself, Eddie."

MORAL OF THIS STORY: If you don't want to be on my mother's Official Shit List, NEVER EVER WALK OUT ON YOUR KID!

Anyway, Quark changed after Mrs. O'Rourke moved to New York. He was always shy and smart, but he just got shyer and smarter, spending all of his free time reading books and messing around on computers. Also, he stopped playing basketball with the other kids, even though he was tall and could knock back threes even then. He still doesn't play with other people—not even me—although I hear his backyard hoop ring when he thinks no one is around.

As for Mr. O'Rourke, he always has a girlfriend. Sometimes several. Once he had three girlfriends at the same time who were all named Ashley. What do you think the odds are of something like that happening? Nothing lasts for long, though. The girls called Ashley come and go.

See what I mean? It's not real hard to understand why Quark hasn't exactly been interested in inviting someone to the junior prom.

Until now . . .

(STILL) ED'S TURN

"You like somebody, Quark? You really, really like somebody?" I ask, sliding him his copy of *Great Love Poems of the Western World* across the table so I won't be tempted to smack anyone else with it.

"That's what I've been trying to tell you," Quark says, still smiling. "I'm in love. With Scout."

"*My* Scout?" My voice cracks, just like I'm in the seventh grade starting puberty again.

Quark gives me a long, cool look. "Technically speaking, Ed, she isn't *your* Scout."

"Of course she isn't *my* Scout. Earth to Quark," I say, imitating Derek Zoolander. "I already knew that. Technically speaking, I'm trying to understand how you can be in love with somebody you don't know."

Quark gives me a dopey, lovestruck grin, which (trust me) is something you don't ever want to have to see for yourself. "I know how I *feel*, Ed."

Coming from Quark, this smarmy bit of standard daytime television dialogue sounds simultaneously canned and weirdly sincere.

"Besides," he says in a chipper voice, "you can fill me in on everything I need to know about Scout. What's her favorite thing to eat, for instance?"

"What? Are you planning to study her feeding habits, then jot your observations down in a lab book?" Even by my supremely low standards, I am being rude. I'm also oddly hostile.

Quark doesn't respond. He just looks bewildered— like a zoo giraffe that accidentally wakes up in the zebra cage and has no idea how he got there.

"I'm sorry, Quark," I say, ashamed of myself. "Okay. Let's talk about Scout and food. The first thing you need to know is that Scout worships food, although you'd never know it to look at her."

The way Scout loves to eat is a joy to behold. Just thinking about her tucking into a Hires Big H combo meal (burger, drink, fries, and special fry sauce) makes me smile.

Quark is looking at me hard. Without blinking, even. "Are *you* in love with Scout yourself, Ed?" he finally asks.

I blast out a laugh so loud it might actually register on the Quark Seismic-Laugh-o-Meter.

"Me? In love with Scout?" I shake my head, thinking of Ellie's hair in the moonlight. "And by the way, stop saying you're 'in love.' Guys don't talk like that. You sound like a freaking idiot."

Eager and willing to be my pupil in the Mysterious Ways of Love, Quark nods to show that he both hears and obeys.

"So. Back to Scout," I say. "She's the greatest. Smart. Funny. She kicks butt all over the soccer field. And as per your original question, Quark, she can easily pack away more grub than any female on the face of the planet and not show it. Chicken wings. Pizza. Curly fries. And another thing about Scout . . ."

"She's here," Quark whispers with widening eyes.

"What?" I feel dazed and confused.

"Scout is here. In the library."

I turn around. Sure enough, Scout Arrington (now appearing in the flesh!) is glancing through a spinner rack full of paperbacks.

Scout's Take

Thanks to my secret built-in Romance Radar, I can walk into virtually any library on the planet and head straight for the paperback romance section without having to humiliate myself by asking a librarian to point me in the right direction.

Today is no exception. Within mere minutes I find my way to the wire racks filled with romances, even though this is the first time I have ever set foot in the Foothill Branch Library.

Amazing, isn't it?

I start riffling through the novels. BINGO! I discover a truckload of books I have not yet read—*Seducing Cecilia*, *The Viscount's Dilemma*, and *Midsummer Madness*.

Whoo-hoo! I have hit the Romance Jackpot.

I pick up *Midsummer Madness* and read the flap copy.

Falling in love with the quick-tempered daughter of his commanding officer had been the furthest thing from Reginald Manwaring's mind . . .

"Scout?"

I look up with a start—and freeze. It's Ed and Quark WALKING STRAIGHT TOWARD ME.

"What's up, Scout?" Ed says with an easy smile that would ordinarily make me go weak in the knees with desire, if my knees weren't already going weak with fear because I've been caught reading romances in public.

I brazenly wave my novel beneath Ed's nose. "Ha! Get a load of this! I'm checking it out for my mom's great-aunt, who's like a billion years old. I guess there's just no accounting for taste."

Ed takes the book from my hand and closely inspects the cover, which makes him shudder. Clearly he's been traumatized by the sight of Reginald Manwaring and Philomena Foxfire dancing in the garden WITHOUT a proper distance between them. Years and years from now, Ed will be having Regency romance cover flashbacks, and it will be all my fault.

Ed quickly hands off the book to Quark, who thumbs through it as though he's actually interested. Naturally, this makes me take a second look at Quark, who raises his eyes and blushes a deep shade of salmon when he sees that I am watching him.

I know EXACTLY how he feels. I'd blush too if someone caught me reading a romance in public, which is why I reach out and give him a friendly little squeeze just to let him know I sympathize.

This time Quark blushes all the way to the roots of his hair.

Ed starts to make a little gargling sound. He snatches *Midsummer Madness* out of Quark's hands and starts whacking him with it.

"Quark!" he says. "Knock it off!"

I'm truly shocked. "Ed! YOU knock it off!"

Ed jams the book into my hand and storms out of the library without saying good-bye. Quark gives me a shy gorgeous smile, then follows Ed out the door.

Okay. I could actually be interested in Quark. I really could. Who knows? It might be fun to watch screwball comedies together. Someone who likes Cary Grant and Katharine Hepburn in *Bringing Up Baby* might be the guy for me. There's only one problem, sadly.

I'm already all gone on his neighbor.

Ed calls me later.

"Two things," he says. "First, I apologize for being rude in the library. Rudeness is a bad thing."

"Poor Quark," I say. "You really gotta stop smacking that boy around."

Ed sighs in agreement, then tackles the second item on his agenda. "I'm serious about getting rid of this gut. Can I go to the gym with you?"

"Sure. I'm going tomorrow," I say casually, but inside I am screaming yes! Finally! She shoots! She scores!

"Can Quark come too?" Ed asks. "He sort of invited himself when I told him that YOU were going to be there."

"No problem."

Like I say, I could have been interested. . . .

From the Lab Book of
Quentin Andrews O'Rourke

I returned (alone) to the library to check out some of the books Scout's mother's great-aunt reads. Specifically, I checked out *The Ungovernable Governess*, *Daughter of the Distant Drums*, and *December Lady*. Then I took them home and read all three of them beneath the floodlight on the deck, where I usually observe the moon.

I thought these books, along with the poems I have been reading lately, would provide me with some useful insight. Instead, they've only confused me.

The women and men in these novels are clearly attracted to one another but they pretend to hate each other. Does this make sense? They stomp around England (usually, although one of the books takes place in Belgium during the Napoleonic Wars), snorting and sniping and glaring at each other until the very end, when they fall into each other's arms and cover each other with kisses that "sear" their skin like "molten lava."

Molten lava?

These people remind me of the characters on my mother's show, which I secretly watch sometimes, and they frustrate me equally as much. Such a waste of time! Energy! Emotional resources! Why won't these characters give honesty a try?

Honesty, if nothing else, has the virtue of being efficient.

Meanwhile, a restless wind blows and a pair of dragonflies tumble by.

JUNe 16

ED'S TURN

A very a) toned and b) tanned girl wearing biking shorts that tastefully complement her black workout bra shouts a greeting at us over the din of the gym. A blond pony-tail on the top of her head bobs as she gives us a huge smile.

"HI! I'M ERICA! AND I'M GOING TO BE YOUR PERSONAL FITNESS ADVISER TODAY! BECAUSE HERE AT BODY, INC., WE WANT TO HELP YOU HAVE THE BODY YOU WANT!"

"CAN I CHOOSE *ANY*BODY I WANT?" I shout back, as I spy a number of very fine female bodies I want and would be more than happy to choose from if given the opportunity.

Scout smacks me. Quark just blinks.

"ABSOLUTELY!" says Erica, her ponytail bobbing like she's starring in an episode of *I Dream of Jeannie*. "MY JOB AS YOUR PERSONAL FITNESS ADVISER IS TO HELP YOU DESIGN A SPECIFIC WORKOUT PROGRAM TAILORED TO MEET YOUR INDIVIDUAL NEEDS SO THAT YOU"— here she points at me and Quark, like she's Uncle Sam on a recruiting poster—"CAN GET THE BODY YOU WANT!"

"RIGHT ON!" Quark says earnestly.

I'm tempted to break Quark's jaw and wire it shut on the spot so he can't say anything for the rest of his life. "Quark! This is not the 1970s and you are not Shaft, which means you are not allowed to say 'right on.'"

Quark may sound stupid, but at least he doesn't look stupid. Give him credit for that. I, on the other hand, look like the very definition of stupid. For starters, my legs are a dazzling shade of hairy white. If my lips didn't keep moving you'd think I was dead, my leg skin is so pale. Also, I'm wearing one of my mom's T-shirts, which I accidentally picked up and packed in my gym bag. So instead of wearing a manly-man T-shirt that says something like "Just do it," I am wearing a girly-man T-shirt that says "Snap out of it!" I've got it on inside out, hoping and praying that people will think I am on the cutting edge of workout wear fashion for men.

"ERICA, SHOW THESE GUYS THE WEIGHT MACHINES WHILE I LIFT, OKAY?" Scout shouts.

Erica (otherwise known as Jeannie) happily bobs her ponytail and commands us (otherwise known as "Master" and "Roger") to follow her. As we thread our way through a thicket of weight-lifting equipment, Quark looks back with naked longing at Scout, who's already at a bench, adjusting for the number of pounds she wants to start off with. I look back at her, too, and suddenly I feel very, very annoyed with Quark.

"Stop ogling her," I snap at Quark, wondering when I started to use high-end verbs like "ogle." "She isn't a piece of meat."

"I am aware of that, Ed." Quark bristles right before my eyes like he's a quaking aspen. "By the way, Ed, you're wearing your mother's shirt inside out."

My spirits start to sink, not unlike the *Titanic* (starring Kate Winslet and Leonardo DiCaprio). If Quark—Quark the guy who once accidentally wore Batman pajamas to school in the second grade—has noticed what I'm wearing, then I'm screwed. No doubt about it. People will stare. They'll gawk. In fact, I feel a pair of eyes gawking at me right now.

I look up—and gasp.

There, hanging on the wall, is a life-sized photograph of Ali! He's cradling a huge silver trophy the size of a punch bowl in his arms, and he's staring straight down at me. Or at least I think he is. As I've said before, it's hard to tell with those sunglasses.

The sight of Ali makes goose bumps pop up all over my arms. Damn! That guy sure does get around!

"IT'S MAJORLY IMPORTANT THAT YOU LEARN HOW TO LIFT CORRECTLY," Erica informs us as she stops in front of a machine that looks like it might have been used as an instrument of torture during the Spanish Inquisition. "YOU DON'T WANT TO PULL YOUR GLUTES, DO YOU?"

"GLUTES?" I shout back.

"GLUTEUS MAXIMUS MUSCLES!" Erica trots out a little gymnasium Latin for our listening pleasure.

"I HATE IT WHEN I PULL MY GLUTES!" says Quark, getting into the spirit of things. He's rewarded by a face-melting smile from Erica. He smiles back.

Dude! It's so obvious. He's secretly practicing smiles for Scout.

I turn back to look at Scout again, completely forgetting to watch Erica demonstrate how to lift properly and thereby putting my glutes in peril.

Scout's lying back on the bench so that her curly hair flows over the sides, her feet planted on the ground. Some guy spots her as she lifts. Whenever he smiles at her, his chest muscles ripple.

"Who's that with Scout?" Quark wants to know, also forgetting to watch Erica the Glutemeister.

"Duh, Quark. How would I know? This is the first time I've been here."

"HELLO!" Erica shouts at us cheerfully. She's jogging in place to keep her heart rate up while talking to us. "ARE WE PAYING ATTENTION? WE DON'T WANT TO HURT OURSELVES, DO WE?"

Quark drags his eyeballs off Scout. He looks so miserable that I actually feel sorry for him.

"Relax, Quark," I say under my breath, while pretending to care what Erica is doing with the machine. "He has WAY too many muscles."

"Really?"

I sense a clear and present opportunity to do some good to my fellow man.

"Women hate guys with that many muscles," I say. "They look like narcissistic freaks."

Quark gives this some thought.

"Then what kind of guys"—Quark does a quick mental search for the right phrase—"do chicks dig?" He gives a nervous little cough. "So to speak. If you know what I mean."

Poor Quark. He should NEVER open his mouth in public. Especially now that he sounds like a refugee from the seventies. And especially now that he's not acting like himself. What's up with that?

"Girls like guys like you, Quark," I say, getting back to the subject at hand.

Quark rolls his eyes in disbelief.

"I'm serious. They like guys who are nice looking. And smart." I sigh a little. "And exceptionally tall."

I hit the jackpot. Quark lights up like a big old slot machine, but only for a minute. Then he narrows his eyes and bores deep eye holes into me. "Are you making this up? How do you know?"

"Call me Herr Doktor Professor Love, Quark," I urge him solemnly. "I know these things because I watch TV talk shows."

Ha! And they say television is a waste of time!

Quark looks hopeful again. He shoots one last look of eternal, undying devotion at Scout and then turns his full attention to Erica aka Jeannie and her instrument of torture. I do the same. Still, for some reason, I'd like to go over there and punch out that smiley guy with the rippling stomach muscles who's helping Scout. It's pretty sick how he's just breathing all over her.

Why do I feel this way?

Because I'm like her big brother, Ben. I'm protective.

Actually, Quark and I ended up having a very decent time, once Erica and her bobbing ponytail stopped trying to get us to sign up as gym members. After she left, we lifted. We watched girls do some kickboxing. We had a juice thing with Scout at the juice-thing bar. In fact, my only bad moment occurred in the locker room, when we were getting ready to leave.

Here's the thing. Guys have this special Y chromosome that makes them want to start snapping other guys in the rear with gym towels whenever they're in locker rooms. It's a proven fact. Eighth-grade males all across America have done science projects that demonstrate this to be the truth.

So. There I was.

In a locker room.

With a gym towel.

Facing Quark's backside.

I think you'll agree that this was a perfect opportunity. I was all alone in the end zone. Quickly I twirled my towel, whipping it into peak optimum snapping condition.

I set up like a quarterback in the pocket.

Yes!

Took aim.

Also yes!

And launched.

Yes again!

"WHAT THE . . . "

Okay. Fine. I admit it. I haven't engaged in serious towel play for a while and my aim was a little off, which is why I accidentally snapped the guy standing NEXT to Quark.

He turned to face me, and I noted with terrified

interest that it was ARNOLD SCHWARZENEGGER!

Just kidding.

The guy looked like Arnold S.

"I'm really sorry, man," I said. And then I said the exact same words again for emphasis.

The locker room went completely silent. As I tried to remember everything I ever knew about the fine art of groveling, the False Arnold looked slowly from me to Quark to me again.

Then he smiled. "Fugeddaboutit. See you guys around." The False Arnold slung a gym bag over his shoulder and left.

See us again? I sincerely hope not! I thought, watching him go.

Pretty much the last thing I want to do in this life is come face-to-face with The Terminator again.

From the Lab Book of
Quentin Andrews O'Rourke

There are times when Ed is truly annoying.

Take today, for example. He accused me of ogling Scout while the three of us were at the gym together.

Naturally, I took offense. I do not "ogle." I have never "ogled." I am not an "ogler." Once again, Ed (who thinks he knows everything) has gotten it all wrong.

I have a confession to make. Sometimes I actually fantasize about punching Ed in the nose, even though he is my best friend. Sometimes I lie in bed at night, thinking about how good it would feel to send Ed sprawling, especially on those days when he's more patronizing than usual.

POW!

Take *that*, Herr Professor Doktor Love!

Then I remember that afternoon in the third grade when I was still attending Uintah Elementary School with Ed.

I was only nine years old, but I was the best basketball player in the third AND fourth grades. I am not bragging when I say this. It's simply a cold, hard fact. I have always been able to recognize a cold, hard fact when I see one.

In fact, I was even better than some of the fifth graders. I was most certainly better than Tommy Knaphus.

I can still see how Tommy looked then, after all these years—his thin, chalk white face spattered with rust-red freckles, his thin, mean eyes, his thin, mean mouth.

Tommy hated that I could take him one-on-one. He hated the way his fifth-grade friends teased him about losing to me, a third grader.

One day, when I was slowly walking home alone—our teacher had made Ed stay late to clean out his desk when she discovered he had some moldy cheese slices in it—Tommy stepped out from behind a huge tree with peeling bark. He'd been waiting.

For me.

"Hey there," he said.

I slowed down, not knowing if I should answer. I kept quiet. I always keep quiet, even when I don't want to.

Even when I want to join in the conversation around me and laugh and talk to people, just like everybody else does.

"Too good to talk to me, huh?" Tommy gave me a little shove. "That's real sweet coming from a kid whose mama just ran away from home."

I froze.

"Do you know why she ran away?" Tommy shoved me again, harder this time. I rocked back on my heels and almost toppled over. "She ran away because her kid's such a stinkin' freak." Tommy bleated out an ugly laugh.

"Shut up, moron!" Ed came running up behind us, his Ninja Turtles backpack bobbing up and down. He flew at Tommy, who was at least twice his size.

"You shut up, Tommy Knaphus! You hear me?"

Tommy's attention shifted from me to Ed. Ed slipped off the backpack and started clobbering Tommy with it.

BAM! BAM! BAM!

Tommy casually threw Ed to the ground—no big deal—but Ed bounced back up like a rubber ball.

"That didn't hurt!" He yelled. Then he started swinging his backpack again.

This happened over and over. Tommy pushed Ed down. Ed bounced back and started up with Tommy again.

Me, I just stood there, hearing in my head what

Tommy had said about me and my mother.

Tommy walked away after a while. He probably got bored picking on third graders. After he left, Ed (whose nose was bleeding by then) turned to me and said, "We got him, Quark! He won't dare mess with us again!"

And he didn't. I didn't give Tommy Knaphus the chance. I stopped playing basketball at recess and when it came time in the fall to sign up for Junior Jazz basketball, I told Dad not to bother enrolling me.

I have never forgotten Ed's reaction that day, though. I've never forgotten the way he went after someone who was going after me.

As I have noted before in the pages of this lab book, I, Quentin Andrews O'Rourke, believe that kindness is important.

And I respect it when I see it.

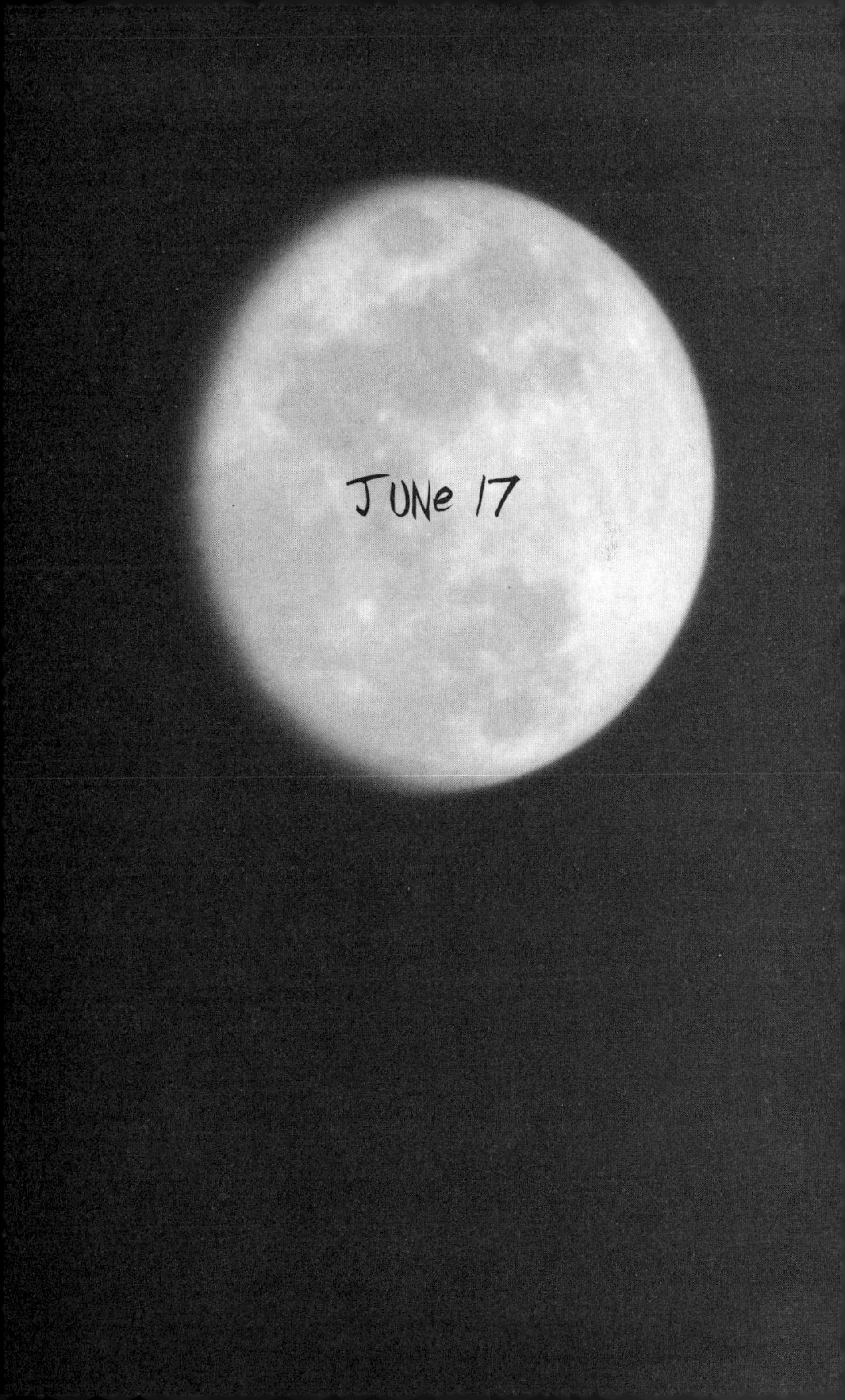
JUNE 17

ED'S TURN

"If you think you're seeing more dragonflies than usual in the Salt Lake Valley this summer, you're right—"

I flip off the breaking dragonfly story on the ten p.m. news and walk out to the backyard so I won't have to listen to Maggie and her girlfriends squealing upstairs. They're having a sleepover, and right now they're playing "Beauty Parlor," which gives them an excuse to put "product" in one another's hair.

I settle into a patio chair and listen to Quark next door, banging shots off the board. Seriously. The guy's amazing. He *never* misses.

A hot, dry wind rustles through aspen leaves and makes me feel restless. Not bored restless. Just *restless*

restless. Full of wanting. Wanting something. Anything. Everything.

The specifics vary, depending on the breeze.

Right now I'm thinking about something I usually try very hard NOT to think about. My so-called date with Stephanie Chandler. I can't help myself sometimes. A wind like this one stirs things up and makes me remember stuff I'd rather forget.

Okay. Let me state for the record that I FULLY understand Stephanie Chandler (don't worry about remembering her name—she won't be back for an encore) is WAY out of my league, so what happened was my own fault, in a way. I'm not a complete moron. I should have known better. I really should have. Stephanie sits on top of the high-school food chain, whereas I'm not even on it.

Still, for some incredible reason, I actually thought I had a chance with Stephanie. Maybe because she was my lab partner in chemistry. Maybe because she laughed at my jokes. Maybe because she smiled at me in the halls when she noticed me.

So I asked her out one day on impulse.

Did you just hear that? I, Ed McIff the Impulsive, actually asked Stephanie Chandler, the Girl Who Makes Male Knees Weaken with Desire, to go out with me.

It was at the end of class, right before the bell rang. I blurted out, "Stephaniedoyouwanttogotoamoviewithmetonight?" She paused. Then she smiled and said sure, why not. So I (walking on air) said I'd call her after school.

Then Stephanie the Beautiful gathered up her books and left.

Later that day I casually told a pal to find someone to go to a movie with, because hey, STEPHANIE CHANDLER AND I would be by to pick them up at seven p.m. sharp!

Man, I really must have been on drugs that afternoon.

I started to get the feeling something was wrong when I called Stephanie after school to confirm times. No one answered the phone. I kept calling her house during breaks from intensive sessions of showering and shaving and making my hair perfect, as well as getting online and buying tickets in advance.

Still, no one answered. Ring, ring, go away. Call again some other day.

It was like all the people in her house were crouched around the caller ID so that the instant my name came up, they could all shout at each other, "FOR THE LOVE OF HEAVEN, DO NOT PICK UP THAT TELEPHONE!"

Finally, with ten minutes left (and counting) until seven, I understood that Stephanie the Desirable and I would not be going out together that night. Or any night.

As Ali would say, it just wasn't in the cards, baby. Different species should not date each other.

So here's what I did: I calmly got into my dad's Hyundai, picked up my friend and his date (by myself), and explained (also by myself) that Stephanie had called at the last minute to tell me she was sick.

Which, of course, was a load of completely nonbelievable crap.

But hey, I was a great sport. I ignored everyone's look of pity and went along to the movie, where I starred as the chaperone.

Later that night, Mom started up with me. Maybe Stephanie hadn't really heard me because the class was too noisy, she said. Maybe Stephanie misunderstood. Maybe there was a family emergency. Maybe her phone didn't work. Maybe she just forgot and then was too embarrassed to call.

Maybe, I said.

Mom finally left my bedroom, swearing like a hockey player under her breath. I'm pretty sure she wasn't swearing at me.

The next day at school Stephanie was her regular, beautiful, way-high-up-there-on-the-high-school-food-chain self. Full of false smiles. Like nothing had happened. Actually, nothing DID happen. That, I believe, would be the point here.

Generally speaking, I choose not to think about this

stuff. I'm sure you can understand my reasons.

It's just that on this restless, *wanting* sort of night, the thing I suddenly want the very most is to forget the sick wave of shame that washed over me when I hung up the phone for the last time and realized that I had been stood up.

Scout's Take

". . . University of Utah entymologist Dr. Elaine Clark says she can't really explain the sudden and mysterious appearance of so many dragonflies. She says it is as though they have flown into town on the wings of a strange wind . . ."

I turn off the evening news (a piece on dragonflies! Slow news day!) and catch sight of my fuzzy reflection in the vacant green of the television screen. I lift a coarse curl, then let it bounce to my shoulder.

I have worn my impossible hair this way—long and loose for years—and lately I've been wondering what I'd look like if I did something different to it. Cut it. Straighten it. Wear it up. Turn it into dreads. Dye it hot pink.

Only I'm too afraid to try something new.

That's me in a nutshell for you. I'm Scout Arrington and I'm afraid.

Surprised? After all, aren't I the one who steps up and wins big soccer games? The one who knocks back straight A's, even in scary subjects like calculus? The one who's involved in a billion trillion activities in school?

Okay. You win. It's true that I do these things. But only because I already know I won't fail.

That's an important point. Did you miss it?

I already know I won't fail!

How totally and completely lame is *that*?

Let me tell you about this dream I have at least two or three times a year ever since I learned to swim. I dream that I am standing on the highest diving platform at the city pool and more than anything I want to jump into the beautiful blue water below. Only I don't. Because I'm afraid I'll do a belly flop and that all the people watching will laugh.

What if the whole world were full of people just like me? People who weren't willing to try something new because they might look stupid. Seriously, what kind of world would that even be? (ANSWER: less messy.)

But so what? *So what?*

Meanwhile, I sit around NOT doing the things I think about doing.

Painting, for example.

Singing.

Making chocolate candy with rum and cherry centers at Christmas.

Dancing.

Flirting.

Writing love poems.

Kissing boys I choose to kiss.

Shouting to the whole world that I don't care what it thinks of me.

Changing my hair.

Disturbing the universe.

Eating a peach.

"Do I dare to eat a peach?" In the poem "The Love Song of J. Alfred Prufrock," that's the question asked by an old man who knows life is passing him by. (BTW, if you haven't read this poem yet, you will. Trust me. It's the kind of poem that makes English teachers salivate, just like Pavlov's dogs.)

I, however, hated the poem. Loathed it. Despised it. Especially the ending, where J. Alfred Prufrock says, "I have heard the mermaids singing, each to each. I do not think that they will sing to me."

On nights like these, when the breezes blow lonely through the trees, I know just how he feels.

Do you know what I want most? More than straight A's and soccer goals?

I. Want. To. Stop. Being. Afraid.

From the Lab Book of
Quentin Andrews O'Rourke

Swish!

Perfect release. Perfect arc. Perfect drop. Perfect shot through the hoop every single time. Sweet!

He doesn't make a big deal about it, but I know my father can't understand why a person (me, for example) would choose to play a team sport (basketball, for example) alone. Naturally he wouldn't understand something like that, because he is the quintessential team player. Football, basketball, and baseball in high school. Football in college. Pickup games of basketball now.

My father can golf like a dream, but he's indifferent to the game. Too much of an individual sport. Besides, golfers don't rough each other up while they're playing.

They don't throw each other to the ground and get grass stains all over their polo shirts, then cheerfully help each other up and slap each other on the behind after the round is over.

What my father doesn't understand is that if you're really good at something (like making baskets) and you don't have other people around to complicate things, you can achieve a sort of perfection. The game stays simple and clean and elegant when you're not playing with someone else.

Swish!

And it's another perfect, boring shot!

I snap up the ball on the bounce, dribble, and spin around. The wind blows, and suddenly I am distracted, even startled by the unexpected sight of dragonflies, dipping in the moonlight.

I go up for another shot and . . . miss!

I didn't just miss. I bricked.

As I chase after the wildly bouncing ball, I wonder with the back of my brain where all those dragonflies have come from. And suddenly I have an epiphany. Right there in the middle of the driveway. Right there in the middle of a summer night. I stop dead in my tracks and just let the basketball roll down the driveway and out into the street as something important becomes perfectly clear to me.

I now understand why I have been dissatisfied, and I

also realize what it is that I really want.

I want people coming at me, trying to put me off my shot.

I want to make a shot in spite of it.

I want heat.

I want dust.

I, Quentin Andrews O'Rourke, *want* complications.

THE EMAIL ELLIE WANTED TO SEND

SUBJECT: What I want . . .

To J.

Mary's boyfriend, Rick, taught me how to say the words in Portuguese.

Eu quero. "I want."

The words look so bold, so naked, so daring and demanding somehow when you say them straight up like that.

Eu quero.

But there they are, dancing through my head as I sit on Mary's balcony in the dark. I came outside hours ago to watch the moon climb over the mountains and wonder if this hurt in my heart will ever go away, when suddenly a single dragonfly appeared. It hovered on glassy wings in front of my face and it was like I could read its mind.

Where are the others? I want the others.

I was so startled, I yelped. Still, the dragonfly hovered so close that I imagined I could hear the hum and feel the flutter of its wings against my cheek. And then out of nowhere—more dragonflies! A whole quivering bouquet of them! My dragonfly darted toward the others, and together they all flew off—straight into the face of the moon. I watched until they disappeared, and then for the first time in a long, long time, I burst out laughing.

Eu quero.

For the months we were together, of course, I wanted you. More than anything. With you I thought I'd finally found what I'd always been looking for—someone who understands me and my dreams.

The truth is, I've never had a lot of friends who were my own age, which is how I know there's something a little "off" about me—that and the fact that I'm the only teenager in Washington County (apparently) who enjoys listening to opera. I'm like that pair of jeans that are a half inch too short to be in style. Close. Just not close enough.

It's not that I haven't tried. I've always done the things people do to make friends—join school clubs, try out for things, say hi to everybody in the halls. But when Saturday night rolls around and I want to do something, I'm the one who always has to call.

"Why don't people like me?" I asked Mom once when I was in the fifth grade.

She pushed my hair out of my eyes. "Everyone loves you, Ellie."

Grandma nodded hard as she stood over the sink, peeling peaches. "That's because you're as pretty on the inside as you are on the outside."

Later that week I heard Mom talking to my teacher, Mrs. Lauritzen, after school. They didn't see me standing there in the class doorway, a soccer ball tucked beneath my arm.

"Ellie says she doesn't have any friends." Mom flashed a quick, apologetic smile.

Mrs. Lauritzen paused—long enough to make my stomach plunge.

"That's not exactly true," she said. "The other children do like and respect Ellie. What I would say is that she doesn't have *close* friends right now."

I could see Mom's face in profile, highlighted by sunlight streaming through the window. She knit her brows together like she was trying to figure out a clue for the crossword puzzle in Sunday's paper.

"Why exactly is that, do you think?" Mom asked. "I know she'd give anything to have a best friend."

I would have, too. A best friend I could always sit by at lunch so I never, ever have to sit down again by someone, not knowing for sure if they were saving the seat for somebody else.

"She will one day," Mrs. Lauritzen said. "Right now they don't know what to do with her because she's very *intense* . . ."

Intense? What did that even mean?

I felt shame spread through me. If I looked in a mirror, I was afraid I'd see an "I" branded in the middle of my forehead.

"Intense." Another word for "loser."

Eu quero.

What do I want this very minute?

I want what I thought I had.

Still wanting,

Ellie Fenn

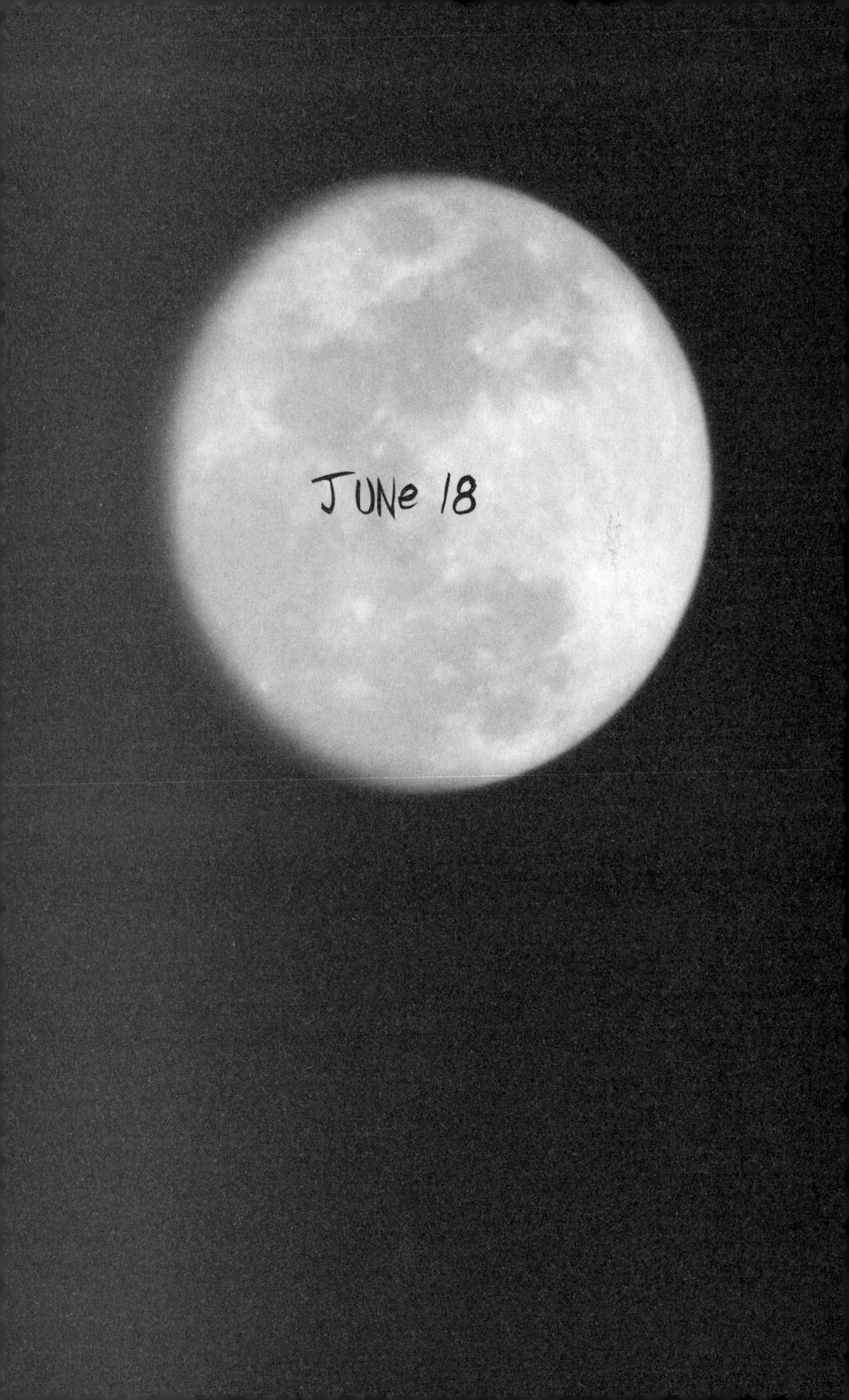
JUNE 18

ED'S TURN

Ellie walks into Reel Life early tonight.

"Hi, Sergio," she says in that voice of hers that's shy and friendly at the same time.

"*Alô*, Ellie," I say. "*Como vai?*"

She giggles a little and answers. NOT in English.

I'm pretty much stunned.

Ellie smiles at me. "You look surprised, Sergio."

No kidding. I probably have the exact same look of surprise that movie stars have when paparazzi cameras go off unexpectedly in their faces. Especially if they've been caught stepping out with their English nanny instead of with the wife.

"That was Portuguese, right?" I ask weakly. Like I

would know anything at all about Portuguese.

Ellie looks pretty crushed. "Is my accent that bad?"

"No!" I rush to reassure her with kindness and also suaveness. "Your accent is *muy, muy bien!*"

Which (technically speaking) is Spanish. But then maybe Sergio is trilingual.

Ellie's face brightens. "Do you really think so?"

"*Sim,*" I say. "I really think so."

She gives a modest shrug. "My voice teacher says I have a good ear for language. But he probably says that to everybody."

"Voice teacher?"

Ellie nods, her eyes shining. "That's one of the reasons I'm here this summer—to study with this amazing, practically legendary teacher who lives here in Salt Lake. I'm studying Italian, too, because you ought to know Italian if you want to sing. I've already taken French and German, but you know how high school classes are."

"*Sim,*" I say again. "I know." Frankly, I feel like I'm being strangled to death by my own bow tie.

"And now that I've met you, I'm getting my aunt Mary's boyfriend, Rick, to teach me"—here Ellie glances over at Scout, who's busy checking in DVDs, and whispers—"some *Portuguese.*"

My stomach drops a little. "Rick? This is short for 'Ricardo,' perhaps? Is this *Senhor* Ricardo from Brazil too?"

Ellie shakes her head. "No. He went on a Mormon mission there—just like Scout's brother. Only it sounds like he's in the north, whereas Rick was in Florianópolis, which is in the south." Ellie looks at me. "What part of Brazil are you from?"

"Somewhere between the north part and the south part," I say. "Most Americans haven't heard of it." Including me.

"Well, Brazil is a huge, amazing country, isn't it?" Again she smiles. "Hey! Maybe you and Rick can meet someday. Maybe you and Rick and Mary and I can all do something together!"

"That would be great!" I say, secretly praying that Ellie will quickly drop the idea of a social hour with me and Senhor Rick.

"Anyway," Ellie continues, "I just wondered if I could hang around the store until you go on dinner break. Maybe we could eat together. I promise I won't bother you until then, Sergio." She glances over at Ali, who is entertaining a customer with a new magic trick. "I don't want to get you or Scout into trouble."

I immediately stop worrying about the prospect of meeting *Senhor* Ricardo. Instead, I nearly do an end-zone victory dance in my frilly Reel Life shirt, right there on the spot.

Ellie is asking me out!

Me!

Ed! Otherwise known as Sergio!

Yes!

Ali gives me a half-hour dinner break, which means Ellie and I will have to chow down fast.

"Do you want to go to Burger King?" I ask. Scout hates BK. She prefers customized burgers, like the Big H pastrami at Hires or the double cheeseburger at B & B Burgers up by the university. Burger King, however, does have the virtue of being fast. And nearby.

"I have an even better idea." Ellie smiles. "Follow me, Sergio."

"I hear and obey," I say.

She leads me out of the store and through the parking lot to a shiny new 4x4 Dodge Ram truck with smoked windows.

"It's Mary's. She let me borrow it tonight," Ellie explains as she unlocks the door, crawls inside the cab, and invites me to join her.

On the seat between us is a very full picnic basket.

"Hey, Boo Boo! Let's grab this pic-a-nic basket and run for it before Mr. Ranger gets here!" I say.

It does cross my mind that cracking Yogi Bear jokes would be something that Ed—not Sergio—would do. But Ellie just laughs and starts up the engine.

"Okay, I figure it will take us five minutes to drive to Liberty Park and five minutes to drive back. If we had more time, we could ride the Ferris wheel there. As it is, we'll have twenty minutes to eat and whatever. Interested?"

"*Sim*," I say. "I'm *muito* interested."

Especially in the "whatever" part.

Although the park is crowded—it's always crowded on a summer evening—Ellie immediately finds a place to dock Mary's truck. Not only that, but we have an excellent view of the pond, which gleams black and silver at twilight.

That is just how incredibly *right* things go for you when your name happens to be Sergio.

Ellie and I get out of the truck and spread a blanket on the grass. Then she reaches into the picnic basket and produces something on a pretty china plate wrapped in plastic.

"Recognize this, Sergio?"

I squint. It looks like a peeled banana with caramel stuff drizzled all over it.

Ellie's face falls a little. "Maybe I didn't get it right. It's a *banana frita* for you. Rick showed me how to make it."

"Of course I know it is a *banana frita*," I say. "My grandmother, she made me *banana fritas* all the time when I was small. I was just too overwhelmed to speak. *Obrigado*, Ellie. Thank you for this *banana frita*."

Ellie smiles broadly. "Rick promised to teach me how to cook all your favorite dishes, Sergio."

The more I hear about this *Senhor* Rick, the less I want to meet him.

Ellie, however, sighs happily as she gives me the food she has prepared with her own hands. She watches me eagerly for my reaction.

"This is terrific," I say over and over, thinking how much Scout would enjoy this meal.

After we finish eating, Ellie leans back on her elbows and looks up at the sky. "It's beautiful tonight, don't you think? Look at those shadows over there, leaping across the grass. It makes me think of things . . . unseen."

Things unseen. I have no idea what Ellie is talking about, quite frankly. But I agree with her anyway. Wouldn't you, if you were me?

I do know this. It's amazing how comfortable I feel right now. If I were still the Dork McIff, I would be asking myself silent desperate questions about sweating: Am I sweating? Is it sweat you can smell or sweat you can see? Or (worst-case scenario) is it sweat you can smell *and* see at the same time?

If I were still Ed, I would be wondering if I should keep my arms at my sides from the elbows up, in case I had sweat stains, and I would also be wondering if my palms were growing unnaturally moist, like stuff growing in a Petrie dish. Sometimes my palms get so wet, you could use them for sprouting things in science classes, such as beans and bacteria.

But now that I am Sergio from central Brazil, I am not worried. Sergio rarely sweats, and when he does sweat, it is a good manly sweat.

"It's almost the twenty-first of June," Ellie is saying. "Midsummer's eve."

She watches the leaping shadows with a faraway look.

"'Over hill, over dale / Thorough bush, thorough brier / Over park, over pale / Thorough flood, thorough fire / I do wander everywhere, / Swifter than the moon's sphere.'"

"Come again?" I say.

She laughs a silvery laugh.

"It's one of the fairy speeches in *A Midsummer Night's Dream*." Ellie sighs happily.

I digest the fact that I'm sitting in a park on a blanket with a beautiful girl who memorizes Shakespeare for fun.

A dragonfly flits by.

"I used to pretend that dragonflies were fairies when I was a little girl." Ellie giggles. "You probably think I'm a total geek now."

"A geek? You? Never."

"Do you like Shakespeare too?" she asks me hesitantly.

"DO I LIKE SHAKESPEARE?" I say. "*Sim!* I *love Senhor* Shakespeare!"

Ellie grows radiant beyond words. "I knew it! Which play is your favorite, Sergio?"

Very fortunately for me, Mrs. Stensrud, my sophomore English teacher, made us listen to a recording of *Macbeth* in class. Also, I read most of the Spark Notes.

"*Macbeth*," I say. And then, for Ellie's listening enjoyment, I toss off a line. "Out, out damn spot!"

"Lady Macbeth." Ellie nods knowingly, then shivers at the thought of that wicked woman caught up in her own deceit, just like an Orc caught in Shelob's web.

Sounds of the growing night wash over us. Ellie reaches for the picnic basket, and without thinking I take her hand.

If I were Ed, I would have pounced on her hand. Clumsily. Like a slobbering overeager puppy pouncing upon a bedroom slipper. Yes, master! Look at me, master! I have your bedroom slipper now, master! Watch me chew it up and shred it into tiny useless bits because I adore you so, master!

But now that I am Sergio, I confidently take Ellie's slim white hand and hold it lightly in my own.

My palms, in case you're interested, are dry. Like the desert. Where Sergio has ridden camels with the sons of many sheiks.

Ellie looks at me. "I just knew there had to be somebody else like—" She stops as though her own words have taken her by surprise. "Somebody exactly like you, Sergio."

And then she kisses me and I almost stop breathing. But not quite, because I definitely kiss her back.

In public.

On a blanket.

In a park.

Beneath a white, rising moon.

Scout doesn't look at me when I return, but Ali actually slides his sunglasses down his nose and fixes me with a stare as I sail through the door.

"What are you grinning about?" he asks.

"I'm grinning because I am just so very happy to be a Reel Life employee, sir!" I say, wondering where I'd suddenly found the courage to smart off in front of Ali. "In fact, I'm so happy to be a Reel Life employee that I feel like doing a little dance to the happiness gods, right here in the middle of your store!"

And I do. Sort of. I sing, sort of, too. "'Do a little dance! Make a little love! Get down tonight! Whoa! Get down tonight!'"

On the "whoa" part I actually drop to my knees and slide across the floor. Or I would if it weren't for the carpet. As it is, I drop to my knees and stay there.

Ignoring me completely, Scout picks up a load of DVDs for shelving purposes and walks to the back of the store. Ali, however, stares at me for a few seconds before coolly sliding the sunglasses back up his nose. Then the most amazing thing happens. A smile breaks out on Ali's face. He gives a long, low chuckle.

"Not bad, McIff," he says.

I spring to my feet like an actor who's just received an Oscar. "Does this mean you like me, Ali? That you really, really like me?"

"Cut the Sally Field crap," he says. "Follow me. I want to show you something."

I follow Ali to the back office. He reaches into his desk and pulls out a deck of cards. He shuffles it quick and clean like a Vegas dealer, then holds it in front of me.

"Pick a card. Any card," he says.

I pull one out from the middle of the deck.

"Now look at it," Ali commands.

Queen of hearts.

"Put it back."

I put it back. Ali reshuffles the deck with lightning fingers, then pulls out a card. He shows it to me.

"Yours?"

Awed and amazed, I nod.

"Queen of hearts, baby," Ali says.

"How'd you do that? That was great!"

He dismisses me with a grin.

"Are you mad at me or something?" I ask Scout as we leave the store after closing up. I always walk her to her car even though she says it's not required—she can take care of herself.

Scout shakes her head no.

Call me psychic, but I'm not convinced.

"You've been avoiding me tonight." I persist.

"I have not."

"Remember that time I called your name, and you turned your back on me? That pretty much looked like avoidance to me."

Scout gets ready to respond, but a horn blares and makes us both jump.

"Scout! Sergio!" Ellie is waving from the passenger window of Aunt Mary's truck. The driver is another very beautiful girl who looks exactly like Ellie, only a few years older. She waves too. Only it's one of those tight constipated little waves that queens in carriages give to peasants shortly before running them over.

FOOTMAN:
I regret to inform Your Majesty that we just ran over another peasant.

QUEEN:
Fortunately for us there are so many more where that one came from . . .

"It's Ellie," I say to Scout. "Let's go over and say hello."

The memory of Ellie's sweet kisses lingers on my lips. Like honey, except not sticky.

"These are the friends I was telling you about, Mary," Ellie says as we approach. "This is Scout and this is Sergio. Scout and Sergio, this is Mary, my mother's baby sister. She's the one I'm living with this summer."

Aunt Mary smiles warmly at Scout, who starts to thaw like a Popsicle right there on the spot.

"Aunt?" I say in the mocha-smooth tones Sergio would use. "You don't look old enough to be an aunt."

Is it just my imagination, or does Mary's smile grow chilly as she turns her attention to me.

"So," she says, "you're the famous Sergio."

"*Sim*," I say. I almost bow but decide that would be over the top.

"What did Ellie tell me your last name is?"

I feel a quick stab of non-Sergio-esque nerves as Scout shoots me a look.

"Mendes," I tell her.

"Sergio Mendes, huh," Aunt Mary says, looking me up and down like a piece of merchandise she isn't interested in.

"Isn't that a scream?" Scout pipes up. She plants a friendly slug in my arm. "I tease him about his name all the time."

Mary keeps looking me over, and I start to feel

seriously offended. What does she think I am? A big phony or something?

"Ellie's been telling me about the two of you," she says finally. "Thanks for being so friendly. I think she's been pretty lonely since moving in with her old-maid aunt."

"That is so not true!" Ellie tells us. "Mary's the best. Anyway, we were just driving around talking tonight when we passed this place, so I made Mary stop and wait. I wanted her to meet you both."

"We'll have you guys over soon," Mary says. "'Night, Scout. 'Night, *Sergio*."

It's like she says my name with italics.

Mary starts up the engine and the truck roars off. Scout and I stand together, watching Mary drive over curbs like she's driving a monster truck.

"She's really nice," Scout says thoughtfully.

I give a non-Sergio-sounding squeak. "Are you talking about Mary?"

Frankly, Mary seems about as nice as your average Roller Derby queen.

"I'm talking about Ellie, duh." Scout slowly turns and looks straight at me. For the first time ever, I see her eyes.

Not that I haven't seen them before. It's just that this time I really *see* them. They're huge and deep brown, except for a strange sunburst of gold right around the irises.

Oh. My. Gosh. Quark is right!

"Listen up, Ed. I am not playing this game where Ellie's concerned anymore. Okay?"

She turns abruptly and stalks off to her car alone without saying good-bye.

So I stand in the parking lot, watching her go, noticing that for the second time this evening, I almost can't breathe.

Scout's Take

She's really nice.

My unexpected words play through my head like a new set of lyrics to the song on the radio.

I'm just driving through the midnight-quiet streets of my neighborhood, wishing like crazy my brother were here instead of in Brazil to help me sort things out. Ben has always understood matters of the heart even though I'm the girl and he's the guy.

Oh, I miss him so much right now I could die, especially on a night like this, when the moon is almost full. I want to hear his soothing Big Ben voice wrap itself around familiar words. "Hand in hand, on the edge of the sand, they danced by the light of the moon."

But Ben is not here. I have to figure this one out for myself.

Here's what I'm thinking so far. I have this gut feeling that if Ellie knew how much I like Ed, she'd step aside for me in a second and yell, "You go!" from the sidelines. Even if she wanted Ed for herself. Which I'm pretty sure she does. Even though she doesn't know his name is actually Ed.

You can see for yourself how confusing this all gets.

Still, I really believe that Ellie is that kind of girl. On the other hand, Ed—my sweet, silly Ed, whom I have known and understood and read like a book for so long—is a total mystery to me right now.

What is going on inside the boy's head?

The Letter Ellie Wrote

Dear Mom and Grandma,

Mary and I had such a blast tonight. We drove her new truck all over Salt Lake Valley. Seriously, I think you should stop giving her grief about how much it cost her, Gran. That amazing truck is worth every penny!

I'm practicing like mad. The singing. The Italian. All of it. I think you'll be amazed at how much I've learned so far! In my spare time I am working on *La Wally*, which I love best of all.

Stop worrying,
Ellie

THE EMAIL ELLIE WANTED TO SEND

SUBJECT: Determined . . .

To J.

By the way, did I tell you? I have met someone who has seen even more of the world than you have. His name is Sergio and he's from Brazil. I do not love him, but I like him and that's a start.

Determined to forget you,

Ellie Fenn

JUNe 19

ED'S TURN

So I was breathless last night thanks to Ellie first and then Scout, and I'm REALLY breathless this morning because stupid Helena the Stalking Cat is purring on the pillow next to my head.

I stagger out of bed and check myself in the mirror. Everything is swollen—my eyes, my nose, my lips, my tongue.

Possibly even my hair.

Swear words fly out of my mouth. As always when she's been caught in bed with me, this is Helena's cue to exit stage left. She jumps onto my chest of drawers, knocks over a mug of pens, and leaps like a nimble little minx out of the window.

But not until she turns her head and shoots me her usual annoying look of undying love.

I swear some more and notice how the blood is pounding behind my swollen eyes. I'm guessing my eyelashes are swollen too.

"You look like crap," I tell my mirror. Then I shuffle across my room and collapse backward onto my bed.

I also *feel* like crap, if you want to know the truth, the whole truth and nothing but the truth—and not just because my head morphed into a lead balloon overnight either. It's strange I should be feeling this way, when you stop to think about it, considering all the unbelievably excellent things that happened to me last night.

Here's the Spark Notes version, in case you've forgotten.

EXCELLENT THING NUMBER ONE: I actually made Ali laugh. *With* me. Not *at* me. Not that I've ever seen Ali laugh at me to my face, but I'm sure he's laughed behind my back.

EXCELLENT THING NUMBER TWO: I was heavily kissed by a girl who looks like she "oughta be in pictures." In a park. On a blanket. In public.

EXCELLENT THING NUMBER THREE: I heavily returned above kisses. All of them.

I almost smile at the ceiling as I remember making out with Ellie. Almost. But not quite.

Not quite? What is wrong with me? AM I ON

CRAZY PILLS OR WHAT?

The phone rings, but I choose to ignore it because I am already busy lying on my bed, feeling like crap.

"Ed!" Mom's voice floats upstairs. "Telephone, sleepyhead!"

I hoist myself off the bed and stumble into the hallway, where I run into the Lovely and Talented Maggie, who wrinkles up her cute little eight-year-old nose at me.

"Boxers," she says, looking at me in my favorite type of evening wear. "Sick."

I pull a face at her as I pick up the phone on the wall. "Hello."

"Hi, Ed."

Yes! It's Scout! The fact that she's calling me first thing this morning makes me strangely happy, especially since I had the feeling she was mad at me last night.

"Are you working today?" she asks.

"Nope. I've got the entire day off."

"I'm covering for T. Monroe this afternoon, but I'm free tonight. Can we get together some place quiet? I really need to talk to you."

I feel a little prick of panic. "Are you okay, Scout?"

A pause. "I'm fine. We just need to talk about something."

"Sure. Sounds good."

"I'll swing by your house on my way home from work," she says.

Scout's Take

Oh now, THAT was totally brilliant.

I've just told Ed I need to see him tonight because I really have to talk to him about something.

Great. Exactly what am I going to say to him? "Ed, I have a crush on you even though you've been such a loser lately!"

I'm not sure, but I'm guessing guys don't really love it when you call them losers. Not even old guys like my grandfather (the one with the scarlet "A" on his chest) like it. Not even when they deserve it. Especially when they deserve it.

What was I thinking? What!

I pick up the new romance (*The Dishonorable Duke*) I

checked out from the Foothill Branch Library the other day, but within minutes I send it sailing across my bedroom.

(If I keep chucking books, libraries all over America will start revoking my privileges. . . .)

ED'S TURN

Scout honks for me around six thirty. She's in her brother Ben's very fine powder blue '69 Mustang convertible. The top is down and the radio is roaring.

I leap into the car without opening the door. I may be just another short white guy, but there is absolutely nothing wrong with my vertical leap, thank you very much.

"Hi, Ed," Scout says, looking even better than usual in her Reel Life uniform tonight. The red polyester bow tie brings out the color in her cheeks. Funny how I never noticed that before.

"Hey, Scout."

She pulls away from the curb and we're off.

"Where are we going?" I ask, grateful that Scout

swerves at the very last second to miss Helena, who followed me to the car hoping to hitch a ride with me.

One thing about Scout. She's a pretty horrible driver. And tonight she's even more horrible than usual.

"I have no idea," she grumbles.

I'll admit that I'm confused right now. Why is Scout grumbling and almost running over cats?

"May I make a suggestion?" I ask, using the same careful tone of voice my dad uses with my mother when she's annoyed with him.

"Whatever."

Scout blasts through a yield sign without checking for approaching traffic (which includes a bus, among other things), and I scream like a little freaking girl!

"SCOUT!"

She slams on her brakes, and I am again grateful—this time for my seat belt, because otherwise I would be doing a face-plant in the windshield right now. Thankfully there isn't a car behind us.

"What is your problem, Ed?" She glares at me.

"You're my problem!" I say, shaken by my near-death experience and also by the sight of Scout's eyes. "Did you even see that bus back there?"

Scout takes a deep breath as she shifts into first gear again. "Sorry, Ed." She laughs a little. "Where should we go?"

"How about Liberty Park?" I say.

☆ ☆ ☆

We're passing through the intersection of Seventh East and Fourth South when I realize that there's been a one-way conversation going in the car and that I've been the only person contributing to it. Scout just stares straight ahead through the windshield, her grip tight on the steering wheel.

"Are you okay?" I ask.

She nods, although I have the unpleasant feeling that she is pretty close to tears. I shift nervously in my seat. What would I do if Scout started to cry on me? Especially if I had no idea why she was crying?

Girls can get like this sometimes. Not that I have a lot of direct personal experience with girls unless they are moms or eight-year-old sisters.

Scout swallows hard, then turns up the radio even louder, thereby lobbing the equivalent of a nuclear bomb into our delightful one-way conversation. Minutes later we arrive at the park. Scout pulls into the south entrance and finds a parking space immediately. It's the exact same space Ellie and I were in last night. It's like I can still smell Ellie's perfume. How weird is *that*?

"Doo-doo-doo-doo!" I perform my personal rendition of the *Twilight Zone* theme song.

Scout looks at me like I am being completely random. I can see her point, so I stop humming.

She turns off the engine and tucks the keys into the

pocket of her tuxedo pants. "Before we get out of the car, I have something I need to say to you."

"I knew it!" I say. "I'm in trouble!"

Scout steals a glance at me, and then she looks down at her hands folded neatly in her lap. I have the feeling she's getting ready to deliver a prepared speech.

"I'd like to thank the Academy—" I say just to help her get the ball rolling.

She looks puzzled. "What?"

"Nothing." I smile at her. "It's okay, Scout. Just say what you have to say."

"Ellie came into work again this afternoon," she says slowly. "While she was there, Ali told me to shelve about a billion DVDs. Anyway, she stuck around and helped me put them all back. If it weren't for Ellie, I'd still be at work right now. I'd probably be at work for the rest of my life."

I let out a long, low whistle of appreciation for Ellie. Nothing stinks like shelving. At least Scout and I get paid for it.

"She's so great, Ed." Scout's words come out in a rush. "She's gorgeous. Nice. Smart, even. I thought she wasn't very bright at first, but that's not true. She's just—innocent. No wonder you like her."

The air around us is suddenly charged with emotion I don't understand.

I remember a stupid story Dad tells about an experience he and Mom had while they were dating. Out of the blue one day Mom asks him who he thinks is prettier—Mom or her best friend, Betty Stuckey. Dad thinks about this, then tells her that Betty has a better face but that Mom (va-va-vavoom!) has a WAY better body.

Mom didn't speak to him for a month.

The point is that I'm sensing I've accidentally wandered into the same kind of minefield good old Dad did all those years ago.

"Ellie's really great." I pick my words carefully. "But so are you, Scout. I mean it."

"Stop jerking Ellie around, Ed. She doesn't deserve it," Scout says, her voice full of passion. "Cut the Sergio crap, okay? Just be yourself."

But I don't like myself, I want to tell her.

I do not speak, however, because I am unexpectedly distracted by the sight of Scout's beautiful pleading eyes.

I really don't know how to describe what happened next. Even now, several hours later, as I sit here in my bedroom holding an ice pack on my throbbing ear as the moon shines through my window, I feel . . . confused. Still. Even more than I did before.

What *happened* tonight? What the hell happened?

So okay. Here's what I did. I promised to stop jerking Ellie around.

Scout shot me a look of gratitude, let out a deep breath, and sank comfortably into her bucket seat. In fact, she suddenly looked as cozy as a cat on a windowsill. A good cat. Not a crazy stalking cat like Helena.

"Well," I said, "don't you look all relaxed."

Scout laughed. "I *feel* relaxed—now that I've had my say."

"You should have your say more often," I said. "You look great when you've just had your say."

It was one of those moments when my brain and my mouth were having one of those little arguments Brains and Mouths sometimes have.

BRAIN:

Stop it. You're talking too much.

MOUTH:

I don't care.

BRAIN:

Keep your thoughts to yourself.

MOUTH:

Maybe I don't feel like it, punk. Ever think about that?

Clearly Mouth was winning.

Scout looked at me, surprised.

"You look REALLY great, in fact. The greatest," I said.

Scout blushed. She got ready to give me a friendly Scout slug in the arm but suddenly stopped herself. She dropped her arm and folded her hands in her lap.

"Are you okay?" I asked.

She turned her head so I could see her face. For one terrifying minute I thought she might start crying.

Crying? What was going on?

Normally I would quote that line from *A League of Their Own* (one of Scout's favorite movies): "Are you crying? There's no crying! There's no crying in baseball!"

But tonight? Well, tonight was not like other nights somehow.

"Come on," I said. "Let's go for a ride on the Ferris wheel."

Scout turned to me. Her eyes were shining, possibly with tears. But there was a huge smile on her face.

On the way over to the Ferris wheel, I bought her a pink and silver balloon. Her hand felt cool and soft when I handed her the string.

When we were on the Ferris wheel, Scout accidentally let go of the balloon. We watched it float higher and higher until it crossed the soft, white face of the rising moon.

"Ed!" Scout gasped, pointing at the sky. "Look."

"Moon light, moon bright, the first moon I see tonight," I said softly.

Scout looked straight at me, her lips parted by soft quick breath.

My heart went bump in the night.

Later, when Scout and I pulled up in front of my house, I didn't want to go inside. I wanted to stay where I was forever and ever. Like a barnacle that attaches itself to the leather seats of vintage cars.

"Want to come inside?" I finally asked. "I'm sure Maggie will be happy to show you her ever-expanding Barbie doll collection."

Scout laughed but shook her head no. I liked the way her curls bounced off her shoulders.

"I have to get up really early tomorrow morning." She sighed.

Still, I didn't make a move to get out of the car. Instead, I just enjoyed how great it felt to be Ed—not Sergio—sitting in a very fine powder blue '69 Mustang convertible with his good friend, Scout.

"Scout, Scout, Scout," I said this like I was saying it for the very first time. "Is that your real name?"

She hesitated.

"No."

"Well, what is it then?"

Another pause. "Aurora Aurelia Arrington. After two pioneer grandmothers. They're buried in the Salt Lake cemetery. Not together, though. I mean they each have separate graves and everything." This amazing information came in a rush.

"Wow," I said.

"I know what you're thinking!" Scout blurted out

miserably. "You're thinking that my name sounds like the name of a heroine in a romance novel and that I'm nothing at all like a heroine in a romance novel."

I blinked in surprise. Where did that come from?

"Actually, I was going to say that your name is a real mouthful," I said.

Scout's mouth popped open. Then she whooped out a huge, husky laugh.

"A very nice mouthful," I added suddenly.

To tell you the truth, mouths were pretty much on my mind just then, and I found myself wondering what it would feel like to kiss Scout.

The evening air between us grew very still. Everything stopped, even the sound of crickets. I leaned toward her. She leaned toward me. I wondered briefly if our noses would bump but decided I didn't care.

To hell with noses, I always say!

So we kissed. It was a real kiss, too. Not a screen one.

When we were through, I leaned back happily in my bucket seat and looked up. I swear the moon winked at me before slipping behind a cloud.

Thank you, moon, I said in my head, *for granting me my wish—a wish so secret and so deep that I didn't know what it was.*

Until now.

"Oh Ed," Scout breathed.

And then she burst into tears. For real.

☆ ☆ ☆

She burst into tears and she tossed me out of Ben's car. Then she floored it all the way down the street, but not before she yelled, "I hate you, Ed! I hate you, I hate you, I hate you!"

She wasn't the only one who felt that way.

The next thing I knew, Quark was leaping over the low hedge between our houses like a giraffe on steroids and coming straight for me. He'd probably been standing out on his stupid front porch the whole time, watching everything.

I squawked in a very non-Sergio-esque way. "QUARK!"

He answered me with his fist. I'm pretty sure he meant to punch me in the nose, but his blow glanced off the side of my face instead.

"Aw, shit, Quark!" I yelped. "You slugged me in the freaking ear."

"TRAITOR!" He spat out the word loud enough for me to hear it in spite of the fact I was rapidly going deaf in one ear. He paused to let it sink in. Then he spewed it at me again. "TRAITOR!"

The word rang to the ends of the street and back again.

I'd kissed Scout. The first girl of Quark's first dreams of first love. The reality of what I'd just done hit me like a hockey puck to the chest.

"Quark," I fumbled. "I don't know what to say."

"I TRUSTED YOU!" He roared.

I looked at him under the streetlight. Shaking. Wild-eyed and wild-haired. Nine years old again. Waiting for his mom to come home.

"Oh, Quark. I'm sorry. I'm so sorry."

I started to pray to God with real intent that Quark would hit me in the other ear. God knew how much I deserved it.

Instead, my best friend did something that hurt even more: He flattened me with one last look full of pain before stalking back into his house.

THE EMAIL ELLIE WANTED TO SEND

SUBJECT: At last. Eyes opened.

To J.

Why wasn't I suspicious?

I should have known that something was wrong when I started lying to my mother and my grandmother—the women who've given me everything, even when they didn't have it to give.

At first I told myself I was just trying to spare them. I was fine! But I knew they wouldn't believe that.

A college boy? I could imagine Grandma saying,

You don't want to get involved with a college boy, Ellie. Not yet anyway.

Mom would worry too. She'd had me when she was my age and she wanted things to be different for me.

So that's why I lied to them that day you and I drove up Snow Canyon to Pine Valley. You wanted to visit Pine Valley because you'd read about it in a guidebook on western ghost towns. The old white church and the pioneer tombstones and the lilac bushes that have bloomed every spring for a hundred years intrigued you. We could spread a blanket and have a picnic and read love poems by Pablo Neruda together.

What high-school boy would think to do that? Whisk me away to a place filled with lilacs and ghosts?

No one I knew.

And what high-school boy would kiss me the way you did after you read to me, make me ache with desire for the sound of words and the feel of you on me like a second skin, both cool and warm?

Same answer.

I told Mom and Grandma that I was spending the day in the canyon with some of my college classmates, and because I had always told them the truth, they believed me.

I also lied to Claire and Maddy when they saw us at the Foodmart on our way there. Remember them?

"Hey!" I waved at them when they burst through the door. "What are you two doing here?"

"Dad has work in Veo, and he told us we could help!" Maddy said with pride. "He's out in the truck, waiting for us."

I turned to you then. "I used to babysit these two when I was in middle school."

"She was our favorite babysitter ever!" Claire said.

"I can imagine," you said, and winked at me. I nearly melted. Then you excused yourself and slipped away to the restroom.

"Who's that?" Claire asked.

I wanted to turn cartwheels and shout out the truth. Instead I said you were a friend from the college.

"Phew!" said Maddy. "I was afraid you were going to say he's your boyfriend."

I laughed. A little too loudly.

"No boyfriends for me, silly girl!" I paused. "But why are you glad he's not my boyfriend?"

Maddy wrinkled up her nose. "Because he's too old."

"He is not!" I said.

"Yeah," said Claire. "He is."

A horn blared outside.

"That's Dad!" Maddy said to Claire. "I'll get the drinks and you get the chips." They scampered away like cats at feeding time.

I stood here, stung. Twenty-two is not THAT much older than sixteen.

Or so I thought.

With eyes wide open,

Ellie

Scout's Take

I told him I hated him. Not just once either. I told him multiple times.

He'll never speak to me again. Ever ever ever.

I strip off my Reel Life uniform and throw it onto the pile of clothes in my closet. Then I flop down onto my bed in my underwear and sob into my pillow.

WHAT IS WRONG WITH ME?

For months I have dreamed of the moment when Ed (finally) looks at me "with desire." And he did. He so so SO did. Tonight. More than once. He even kissed me as we sat together listening to Annie Lennox purr "Love Is a Stranger" on the radio in Ben's car.

Okay. Before I go on here, I want to stop for a minute

and think some more about The Kiss. I'll leave it to the romance writers to fill you in on the mechanics of the thing. Instead, I want to concentrate on how it made me feel.

Ed's kiss was like eating raspberries straight from the garden—sweet and hot as the summer sun—raspberries that burst on your tongue and stain your lips with scarlet juices so that you can still taste the memory of the fruit long after the fruit is gone.

I love raspberries and I loved Ed's kiss, which made me feel strong and beautiful.

UNTIL IT MADE ME FEEL GUILTY.

And now I understand why I told Ed that I hate him—he made me forget all about Ellie.

Here's the part I didn't mention when he looked at me "with desire." While Ellie and I were shelving DVDs, she said she thought it would be fun if the two of us started hanging out and asked for my cell phone number and email address. Then she confessed to me that she might like Sergio, otherwise known as Ed.

So what would you do if someone shared a secret like this with you? Would you go out THAT VERY NIGHT and start kissing THAT VERY BOY?

And here's another thing.

I hated Ed because after all these months he has finally given me what I wanted.

And now I am even more afraid.

FROM THE LAB BOOK OF QUENTIN ANDREWS O'ROURKE

References to the moon turn up in the most unlikely of places.

For example. I was flipping through a book of poems tonight and found the archaic term "moon-cursor," which comes from the seventeenth century.

The footnote explained that a moon-cursor was a decoy—a boy who offered to lead travelers to safety by the light of his lantern on moonless nights. Only instead of taking them to the nearest inn, the moon-cursor led them straight to a gang of thieves waiting to rob them.

Moon-cursor.

Thy name is Ed.

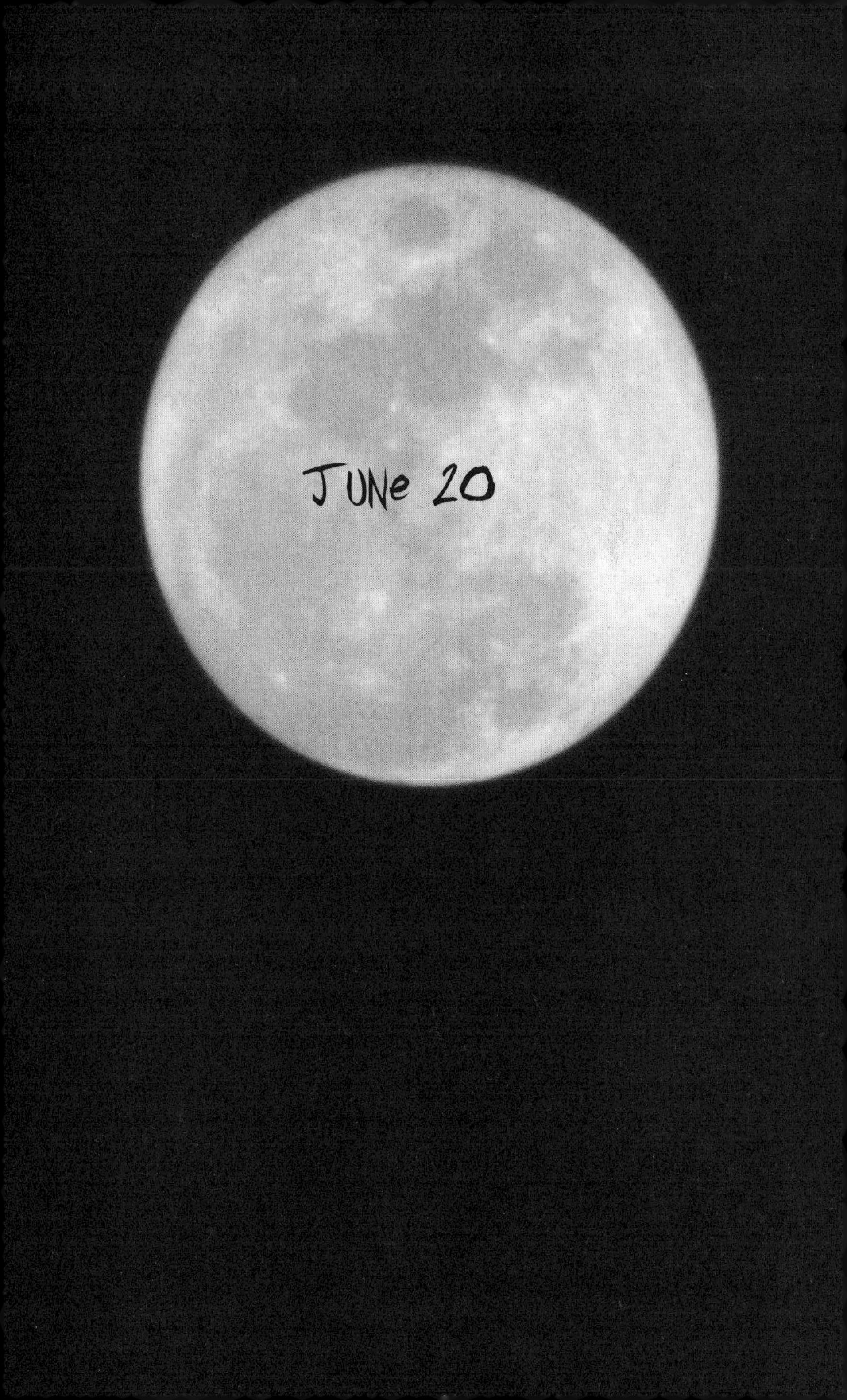
JUNE 20

ED'S TURN

So here's how things stand when I go to work: Both of my best friends totally hate my guts.

Gee. Ain't life grand?

I punch in and check the schedule to see if Scout is working with me. She's not, and to tell you the truth, I am really glad. I definitely need some time to figure stuff out.

Unfortunately, I am working with T. Monroe, who's telling me (again) about the time he turned himself into the police when he discovered he was going five miles per hour over the speed limit in his minivan.

"Really, T. Monroe?" I say to him through clenched teeth. "I didn't think it was aerodynamically possible to break the speed limit in a minivan."

At the moment I hate T. Monroe for being such a self-righteous minivan-driving moron.

As you can easily tell, I'm having a very bad day—a bad day that only gets worse. Remember that guy in the locker room who I snapped with my towel? The guy who looked exactly like Governor Arnold Schwarzenegger? The guy I hoped to never ever meet again in this life? Or the next?

SURPRISE!

Well, he just sauntered into the store. No kidding.

The false Arnold strolls casually to the counter where I am working and gives me one of his false-Arnold smiles.

"I'm looking for some dude named Sergio." He says this like he's issuing an invitation to a rumble. It'll be me and him and our boys. The Sharks and the Jets at Pioneer Park on the west side of Salt Lake City. Midnight.

I gulp, hoping he won't recognize me. "I'm a guy named Sergio. See? It says right here on my name tag."

The smile stays on Arnold's face, but his eyes narrow as he holds out his boxing glove of a hand. "I'm Rick. Mary and Ellie's Rick. I understand we've both done time in Brazil."

Rick. *Senhor* Rick.

My stomach drops like a loose elevator on its way

straight to the cellar of a very tall building. I cannot believe this. Rick is False Arnold—the guy I once assaulted with a wet towel.

"Pleased to meet you, Rick," I lie, offering my hand. Rick casually takes it, mangles it, and returns it to me— a mere shadow of the hand that it used to be.

"*Como vai?*" he says, leaning across the counter so that his face is just inches from mine. I feel his hot breath.

Lucky for me, I've been prepped for this one. "Oh you know. Same as always."

Rick pulls back a little and studies me like I am material for the world's easiest pop quiz. He rattles off line after line of fluent Portuguese, then finishes up with an easy smile.

"*Sim,*" I say. I attempt to laugh lightly, but instead I accidentally make a snorting noise. Also, I am sweating. Heavily, like Ed and not like Sergio.

"*Sim?*" Rick's eyebrows shoot up in mock confusion. I nod.

"But I didn't ask you a yes-or-no question. I'm afraid I don't understand what you mean."

But of course he does understand. Perfectly.

Just my luck. The United States of America is probably full of amazingly stupid bodybuilders who don't speak a single word of Portuguese. Why does Mary the Big, Bad, Mean Roller Derby Queen have to know a smart one?

LIFE IS SO UNFAIR.

"Houston," Rick says, cracking his oversized knuckles, "we've got a problem."

"*Apollo 13.* Tom Hanks. 1993." I buzz in with the correct response. If I were handing out Oscars, I'd present one right now to *Senhor* Rick for Best Adaptation of a Famous Screen Line for Personal Use.

Rick chooses not to be diverted by my friendly game-show banter. "Mary asked me to check you out, *Sergio*." He pauses for dramatic effect. "I guess she has a right to be suspicious."

I don't say anything, just bow my head like some poor stupid dog who knows he's gonna get the crap kicked out of him by Arnold S.

Rick shoves his Arnold S. face back into mine. "I don't know what game you're playing, dude, but I want you to count Ellie out."

I swallow and nod, fear and shame coursing through my veins like salmon swimming upstream.

"I'm giving you a choice," Rick went on, "because I'm fair like that. Either you come clean with her, or I'll do it for you. Okay?"

"I'll tell her myself," I say.

"Is that right? Well, I'm the kind of guy who appreciates details," Rick says. "Exactly when will you clear up this misunderstanding?" He cracks his knuckles again, which reminds me of bones breaking.

My bones.

"This afternoon," I promise. No birds like stars then. No picnics with *banana fritas* for dessert. No moonlight.

I stand up straight, square my shoulders, and look Rick straight in the eye. "Tell her to come by. I get off work at four."

Rick nods slowly. "Okay then." He backs up and looks me over. Is it just my imagination, or do I see a glimmer of respect in his eyes?

Nah. It's just my imagination.

"We're protective of Ellie, Mary and me," Rick says. "You aren't the first guy that's lied to her."

"I'm sorry," I say.

"Seems like I've heard you say those words once before," says Rick. "You had a gym towel in your hand that time."

Can this possibly get any more humiliating?

"Apologize to Ellie," Rick said. "And if you don't, I want you to remember something."

"Yes?"

"I'll be back. . . ."

It's a couple of minutes before four, and T. Monroe is asking me if I think it's blasphemous for a believing person (like himself) to watch actors (probably sinners) portray Christ (definitely not a sinner) on the silver screen.

"I wouldn't know," I say. "I try not to think about

stuff like that, and frankly I think it would be better for your mental health if you didn't either. You're driving yourself crazy over phantoms, T. Monroe. Save your guilt for something real."

"Such as?" he huffs. Clearly T. Monroe does not want to be beaten in the Guilt Derby.

"SUCH AS SCREWING OVER INNOCENT PEOPLE WHO TRUST YOU!" I snap. "NOW THAT'S A REAL SIN!"

I'm on edge, as you can clearly tell.

"Hi, everybody!" Ellie breezes through the door as if on cue, bathing both T. Monroe and me in one of her radiant Ellie smiles.

T. Monroe looks like the heavens have parted and he's just seen a vision. He greets Ellie, full of Christian love and fellowship.

I smile weakly at Ellie, conscious of the fact that she won't be wanting smiles from me soon enough. "I gotta punch out and then I'll join you. We—we need to talk."

Ellie gives a light, unconcerned shrug as she twirls her beautiful long hair with her beautiful long fingers. For all she knows, I could be planning to ask her if we could swap *banana frita* recipes.

"Rick said you wanted to see me about something," she says.

I swallow and nod (also weakly), then leave her standing with T. Monroe while I fly to the back office to punch out. I throw open the office door and jump—eek!—in surprise. I thought Ali was gone, but here he is sitting at his desk.

He swivels around. Deliberately and slowly. For the first time ever, he takes his sunglasses completely off to look at me, only I get the distinct impression that he's looking *through* me—directly into the dark heart of Ed McIff, where strange and unknown evils lurk.

I turn away from his gaze and find my time card.

"What are you about, baby?" he asks as I punch out. His voice sounds like distant thunder rolling down Mount Sinai.

I slip my time card back into its slot and turn around to face him. Also deliberately. Also slowly. I look at him straight. Eye to eye. *Ojo a ojo.*

"I'm getting ready to take care of a little personal business, Ali," I say. "I'll see you tomorrow night at the party."

He nods like he's not sure he believes me and returns to business of his own.

From the time Rick left until the moment Ellie walked through the door, I have been stewing about how to tell her the truth. Should I buy her a nice dinner first, then break the news? Or should we go for a walk, possibly past a grocery store where I can go inside and buy her a rose from the cooler? Should the two of us return to Liberty

Park, where we can remember our first kiss and also feed a few ducks?

Would any of this make her feel better?

Or am I just stalling?

As soon as we walk outside into the parking lot, I decide to tell her the sorry truth and get it over with. A hot breeze picks up and an empty Burger King bag skitters past our feet. I sigh. Telling her the truth beneath a remorseless sun in a parking lot seems appropriate somehow. A dreary setting for a story with a dreary ending.

"So what did you want to tell me, Sergio?" Ellie asks, her face glowing. She reaches out and tenderly smoothes back the hair that has fallen into my face, and I realize that I am truly hating every guy who has ever lied to her—especially myself.

I take her wrist gently and hold her eyes with mine.

"Ellie, I am a fraud."

She's still smiling, but confusion steals like a cloud across her sunny summer face.

"My name isn't Sergio. It's Ed. Ed McIff."

"But your name tag . . . ," she falters.

"It belonged to someone who worked here before I did."

"So you're not really from Brazil," she says slowly, tasting the bitter implications of her words.

I shake my head. "No, although I know somebody

who lives in Brazil. Ben. Scout's big brother." Like THAT matters. I give it a try, however, because I am just desperate enough to fill the chasm growing between us with talk, no matter how lame.

"So," she begins, "you don't really speak Portuguese?"

"No. But I would like to." Like THAT also matters.

Ellie's arms are folded tight against her chest as though she's protecting herself. From me. She stares at the ground.

"Why did you lie to me?" she asks, still looking down.

I cut directly to the chase. "Because—because I'm a jerk."

Although her head is still bowed, Ellie raises her eyes, and I go on.

"When you walked through the doors that first night, I thought you were the most beautiful girl I'd ever seen, and when you noticed my name tag—well, I decided to go for it. I turned into Sergio."

Ellie thinks about this. "How do you know I wouldn't have liked Ed just as much as I liked Sergio?"

I let rip with a ripe royal snort. "Give me a break."

She looks at me with surprise.

"Girls like you don't notice guys like me."

For a split second, Ellie looks wounded—like she's been smacked hard across the face. Then she recovers.

"You may think you know all about *girls like me*," she

says, biting off each word. "But that's not the same thing as actually knowing *me*, now is it?"

No doubt about it. An icy breeze is blowing my way.

"Who knows?" Ellie says. "Maybe I could have walked through the door and thought you were pretty cute. Maybe I could have said, 'Your name is Ed? Well, I'm Ellie Fenn from Santa Clara, and I'm very pleased to meet you!' Maybe you could have said something funny and made me laugh and maybe you would have laughed, too, in which case I would have noticed that you're even better looking when you smile, that actually you have a smile to die for. Maybe we could have been friends. Maybe we could have been more. Maybe.

"But now we'll never know how it could have been between us, will we, *Sergio*?"

She spins sharply on her heel and walks off without looking back.

As final exits go, it's absolutely perfect—controlled, well-timed, brutally elegant.

So this is what I do. I start to walk and I do not stop, and as I walk I take a good hard look at all the scumbag things I've been up to lately. Here's a list in case you want to review for a quiz later.

1. Lying to Ellie.
2. Making Ellie fall in love with Sergio.

3. Two-timing Ellie with Scout in her brother's Mustang convertible.
4. Kissing Scout after Quark has confessed that he himself is in love with Scout.
5. Making Scout furious enough to toss me out of her brother's Mustang.
6. Shooting Bambi's mother.

J/k about Bambi's mother. Even I'm not that bad. Not yet.

Slap. Slap. Slap.

My shoes pound the ground as I walk down sidewalks and across streets. The hot sun sits on the horizon like a white all-seeing eye, staring down on me (the Guilty One) so that my lovely frilly white shirt is soon soaked in sweat. Ed sweat.

An old Firebird with a throbbing stereo slows down. Someone inside shouts something at me in Spanish, then follows up by making little kissing noises. Everybody laughs. Ha! Ha! Ha! The car, still vibrating with bass, peels off and leaves me and my limp frilly shirt in the dust.

That's when I look up and notice where I am—in the heart of Salt Lake's Central City neighborhood where the phrase *Se habla español* appears on most of the signs.

And that's when I notice the shrine next to the bus stop.

I've heard about the shrine on the news. About two or three years ago, the city decided it was a lawsuit waiting to happen and made a move to shut it down, but so many people protested that the mayor backed off. Now here it is, right before my naked eyes.

The shrine is actually this huge old tree where the image of Jesus supposedly appeared. Some of the local residents were pretty excited about this event and built a little platform around the tree's trunk so that people can get a better look at the exact spot where Jesus showed up. There's also a small covered bench for kneeling and praying in front of the tree, as well as two low tables covered with burning candles that flicker in the breeze. Everything is covered with faded pictures of Jesus and Mary, as well as garlands and bouquets of pink and orange and yellow plastic flowers. There are other things, too, like balloons and stuffed animals and old school photos—things a kid would leave if he wanted to give Jesus a present so that Jesus would do him a favor in return.

It's the kind of place you don't expect to find in the heart of downtown Salt Lake City. It's the kind of place where Sergio, lonely and homesick for the hot air of Brazil, would probably feel comfortable.

So I stand awhile in front of the shrine, just looking at all the pictures and the flowers and smelling the thick scent of burning white candles. Then I notice the undershirt tucked between fistfuls of flowers. It's very small, with snaps on the side—the kind that brand-new babies in the hospital wear.

Suddenly I find myself wondering about who had left it and when and why, and before I know it I can see the whole thing like a movie in my head—a mom and a dad leaving the tiny undershirt at the tree, making all kinds of promises to God so that their baby will be okay.

Sadness burbles up inside of me. Probably it wasn't the parents' fault that the baby had problems. Probably that baby was born with some condition—like a hole in its heart, for example. That's what happened to my second-grade teacher's baby boy. It wasn't anybody's fault, she explained to us after. Sometimes stuff like that just happens in life.

ON THE OTHER HAND, there are certain things in life that are definitely a person's fault. I think of Ellie. Scout. Quark. Remember their faces. Feel my sadness turn to remorse.

Out of the blue it's like I hear Jesus-in-the-Tree doing a voice-over in my head.

You hurt them, Ed.

I bow my head a little—enough to be respectful but not enough to look like I've suddenly morphed into T. Monroe. I say a prayer.

I promise to make it up to Scout and Quark and Ellie. I promise to make them happy.

THE EMAIL ELLIE WANTED TO SEND

SUBJECT: Déjà vu

To J.

How did this happen again?

Will I be like Mom's coworker LaDawna Ashton Young Dewey Niilsen Dewey (she married the Dewey husband twice) Woodruff, who keeps marrying different versions of the exact same jerk? Each time she says, "But this one's different."

WHAT IS WRONG WITH ME?

I found out about YOU by accident late one night at the college library. I'd stopped there on my way home from the mall so I could dash in and check out a book.

At first I couldn't believe it was really you, hidden in a corner behind the stacks. I almost waved and called out your name. *Hey you! I thought you said you were working tonight!* But then I realized you weren't alone.

I heard her laugh first—a low, throaty laugh. And then I saw her lean into you and you cup her eager face in your hands.

I headed straight for the bathroom. Locked myself in a stall. Threw up until I was dizzy. And then I cried.

I thought about confronting you that very night beneath the blooms of apricot and almond trees. I wanted you to comfort me, tell me I'd gotten everything wrong.

But it was already too late. Your mask had slipped away and I had seen you for who you really are.

Angrily yours,
Ellie Fenn

Scout's Take

Surprise!

When I'm online this morning, Ellie IMs me.

ELLIE: Hey, it's me, Ellie.

Seeing her name pop up makes me feel all guilty, like I've been caught checking out Regency romances from the library by my AP English teacher. I cannot believe I let Ed kiss me. That I wanted him to kiss me. That I *still* want him to kiss me, even though I hate him with all my heart. WHAT IS WRONG WITH ME?

ME: Hey, Ellie, what's up?

ELLIE: Not much. Just wondering if you want to do something later. I finish my voice lesson at 5.

Ali's party is tonight. I don't think I'll go, though. I

can't avoid Ed for the rest of my life (sadly), but at least we don't have to bump into each other at the same social events.

ME: Sounds great!

Stupid Ed. He's ruined EVERYTHING. First my life. Now Ali's party.

ELLIE: What should we do?

Last year Ali hired Mazza restaurant to cater. I still think about the baba ghanoush and how great it was. No kidding. My mouth is watering right now. I love baba ghanoush. I LOVE ALI'S PARTY.

ME: Maybe we could go to the dollar movie.

The dollar movie? Now there's a brilliant idea— watching someone else have a life instead of having one of my own. Stupid Ed! Why should I miss out on baba ghanoush when he's the one who's been acting like an idiot?

ELLIE: Sounds fun. Which one? What time?

Maybe Ed won't go to the party. If he has any decency at all he'll stay home. And if he's there, I'll totally ignore him. Meanwhile, I can introduce Ellie to a few more people.

ME: How about this instead. There's a party at Ali's house tonight. . . .

ED'S TURN

It's Thursday night—the night of Ali's Midsummer Eve's Costume Ball. Helena the Stalking Cat is sitting on my dresser, watching me get ready. Normally I would have tossed her out the window by now, but I don't want to alienate the very few friends I have left. Even the ones I'm allergic to.

"Thank you, Helena," I say, "for loving me in spite of myself."

She gives me a yellow-eyed, blissed-out purr.

I don't even know if Quark is still planning to go with me to the party. We haven't spoken since he decked me in the ear.

The phone rings as I pull on my Starship Enterprise

uniform, which I found "reduced for quick sale" at the the Costume Shoppe on Thirty-third South.

I fumble for the receiver. "Hello?"

It's Mr. O'Rourke. "Quentin wants me to tell you to be ready at nine p.m., Ed. He'll drive."

"If you're calling, he must not be speaking to me yet," I say.

"I don't know anything about that," Mr. O'Rourke lies smoothly.

"Quark's a stand-up guy," I say. Not everyone would go to a party with someone they weren't speaking to. Quark, however, would go out of a pure sense of duty. "Please let me talk to him."

I hear Mr. O'Rourke say in muffled tones, "For Pete's sake, hold still! I'm almost done." He gets back on the phone and says mysteriously, "Ed, Quentin can't talk right now. . . ."

All is made clear when Quark honks out front and I join him. He's sitting in his car, wrapped in gauze bandages from head to toe. The only actual body parts I can see are his eyes and a little bit of his nose.

"You missed part of your left nostril," I inform him.

"Mmmmmmmmmmmmmm," Quark says, which (no doubt) means "piss off" in ancient Egyptian.

I should have guessed that Quark would show up dressed like a mummy. He was always a mummy for

Halloween, whereas I was always a ninja.

"Okay, Quark," I say as we hurtle down the street, "I've got two very important things I want to say to you before you get us killed. The first is that I'm sorry I kissed your girlfriend. That was wrong of me to do. Wrong, wrong, wrong. I'm sorry for acting like such a jerk."

"Mmmmmmmmmmmmmmmm," says the mummy to my left.

"The second thing I want to say is that I am going to do everything in my power to bring you and Scout together. It's my new mission in life." I pause for a minute to let my words sink through all those bandages. "Scout will be there tonight, by the way."

Scout. Saying her name is like taking a knife to the heart.

I sink back in the passenger seat, hoping that nobility will feel really great.

Only it doesn't. Being noble pretty much sucks, actually. But you know how it is: A Klingon's gotta do what a Klingon's gotta do.

Scout's Take

There are cars up and down the street when Ellie and I arrive at Ali's house. We drive around the block a few times and finally park around the corner. Neither one of us gets out of Ben's Mustang right away, however, because we've been having so much fun just talking.

Who knew a thing like that could happen? Just goes to show how deceiving first impressions can be.

"Look," Ellie finally says, settling back against the bucket seat, "I want to tell you that I know all about 'Sergio.'"

She makes little quotation marks with her fingers when she says the word "Sergio."

I cover my face with my hands and groan with shame.

"I am so sorry I didn't tell you the truth." I peek at her through my fingers and discover she's smiling. "How did you find out?"

Ellie tells me the story, and I groan again. Trust Ed to break the news to her in the parking lot. What do I see in this boy?

Ellie laughs. "It's okay, Scout. I promise. When he told me yesterday afternoon, I was so mad I just wanted to grab him and pull out all his hair and—oh, I don't know—punch him in the face over and over."

"I don't blame you. Ed makes me feel that way too, sometimes."

"After I cooled down last night, I had to admit I hadn't been completely honest with him either."

I won't lie—I felt something like hope stir inside me. Hope. Can you believe it? In spite of everything?

"What do you mean?"

Ellie sighs. "I was distracting myself with Sergio in the hopes of forgetting somebody else."

Then she tells me the true and terrible story about the college boy who broke her heart.

Even though the night air is warm, Ellie shivers and wraps her arms around herself like a cloak of flesh. "What is wrong with me, Scout? You'd think I'd learn."

I feel completely sick inside. And, say what you will about Ed, if he heard Ellie's story, he'd feel sick inside too.

ED'S TURN

Fourth Avenue is clogged with cars. Clearly, half the population of Salt Lake City has shown up for Ali's stupid Midsummer Eve's Costume Ball. It's hard to believe no one has complained about this party to the cops over the years. Quark manages to squeeze into a space between T. Monroe's minivan and a rusted hunk of junk plastered with bumper stickers that say things like MEAT IS MURDER and MY KARMA JUST RAN OVER YOUR DOGMA.

Quark and I climb out of the car and start walking toward Ali's midnight blue, mosaic-covered house (which is straight across the street from the old Salt Lake Cemetery) when I make two equally terrible discoveries, thanks to a pair of very fine-looking girls who are currently ringing Ali's doorbell.

First Terrible Discovery: THE GIRLS ARE NOT IN COSTUME. Neither are the people who greet the girls at the door. Suddenly I have a Midsummer Eve's epiphany.

DUH! THIS ISN'T A COSTUME PARTY!

I'm sure you've all had the experience of showing up some place wearing a suit, only to discover that everybody else is wearing jeans. Actually, you probably haven't. But I have. Mom made me wear a suit to my friend Jacob Kahn's bar mitzvah party.

Mom didn't know the first thing about bar mitzvah parties, okay? Probably because she grew up on a potato farm in southern Idaho, where there are just not a lot of bar mitzvah parties going on. The only thing Mom knew is that she wanted us to be respectful. So she made me wear the same suit I wore (respectfully) to my grandfather's funeral earlier that spring.

I'll never forget how I felt when I walked into Jacob's house and saw all those kids wearing T-shirts and Nike shorts, waiting for the party to start.

"Dude!" one of them shouted. "You're going bowling in a suit?"

I wanted to walk straight into the bathroom and stick my head down the toilet.

Anyway, I'm having SERIOUS déjà vu all over again in front of Ali's house. Hey!

How could I have gotten this so wrong? How could I have gotten everything so wrong?

I start to make little strangling sounds, while Quark becomes supremely agitated. He jumps up and down and flaps his bandage-swathed arms around like he's trying out for head cheerleader.

"Mmmmmmmmmm! Mmmmmmmmmmm!" he says, which is how you express extreme agitation in Ancient Egyptian.

"Jeez! Stop bending my ear, why don't you, Quark!" I snap. "A Klingon can't hear himself think with you yakking all the time!"

Time to think is exactly what I need, too. I have to formulate a quick plan because of the Second Terrible Discovery I have just made. You know those very fine-looking girls not wearing costumes who just walked into Ali's house?

Well, one of them for sure is Scout. Scout as in my-best-friend's-would-be-girlfriend-even-though-I-want-her-for-my-own-girlfriend Scout. I'm serious. I would recognize that amazing hair anywhere. And although I didn't see the other girl's face, I think it might be Ellie.

Ellie? Scout? Ellie and Scout together? When did *those two* get to be such good buddies?

"Look, Quark," I say. "I am NOT going in there dressed like this, so let's just turn around and go home right now. Who cares if Ali fires me for missing his party?"

I'm assuming here, of course, that beneath all his bandages, Quark feels the exact same way I do at this moment, which is that I would rather do combat *mano a mano* with a rogue Romulan officer rather than have the Girl of our Mutual Dreams (that would be Scout) see us dressed up in our Dork Clothes.

I make a move to leave, but Quark stays rooted to the spot like a tree. An extremely stubborn, mummified, Ancient Egyptian tree.

"Quark!"

He ignores me because he's so very busy staring at the front door through which our MDG (Mutual Dream Girl) just walked.

I grab his arm, but Quark shrugs me off. Then he stomps stiffly toward Ali's house like he's Franken-freakin-stein.

"DUDE!" I shout after him as he clambers up Ali's front steps. "LIVE IN THE NOW! SCOUT DOES NOT WANT A BOYFRIEND WHO'S BEEN DEAD FOR FOUR THOUSAND YEARS!"

Quark ignores me. He doesn't even look back, which is hard for mummies to do under the best of circumstances because of all those neck bandages. And these are definitely NOT the best of circumstances.

The next thing I know, Quark enters the Secret Chambers of Ali (otherwise known as Ali's house) and disappears from view.

I spit out a Klingon swearword I found online: "guy'cha'" (which, for the record, is the stronger form of the more polite "ghay'cha'").

And suddenly I find myself engulfed by an enormous tsunami of approaching guests, including this lady with a hairy little dog who tries to bite me even though she doesn't have any teeth left. (The dog. Not the lady.)

Against my will, I am swept along inside.

For obvious reasons, it doesn't take me long to spot Quark in Ali's living room, which looks completely amazing. There are candles and strands of colored motion lights and paper lanterns. The air is thick with the sound of steel drums and the scent of spices.

There are people EVERYWHERE.

In fact, I have never seen so many people at a party. Different kinds of people too. You know how it is at most high school parties—jocks go to jock parties, braniacs go to brainiac parties, Klingons go to Klingon parties.

But here in Ali's house it's different. There are kids and parents, young guys with dreds and old guys with no hair, women my mom's age wearing sweatsuits, skaters wearing jeans weighed down by heavy chains, men dressed like men and men dressed like women (okay, there's only one guy here in a skirt).

Ali's guests look like a collection of strangers standing together in a line at Disneyland, but here everyone is actually in a good mood—talking and sharing food and laughing, too, in spite of the fact it's so crowded. Take this sweet little old lady standing next to me, for example. She's speaking Dutch to a guy with a boa constrictor (I'm not lying) wrapped around his big thick neck. And across the room I see T. Monroe (and his mother) chatting happily to a tall thin girl dressed in drapes of black velvet accessorized by jewel-encrusted crosses. She holds a single white lily and beams like the Virgin Mary at T. Monroe.

The doorbell rings. One of the "mom" ladies answers the door.

"Why it's the missionaries!" She squeals. "Come inside right this minute and I'll get you something to eat. My oldest son is serving in southern Belgium. . . ."

About the only thing I DON'T see is another person dressed up like a Klingon. Everybody else (not counting me and the Mummy Quark) obviously came as himself or herself—no matter how different that self might be.

I blush with hot shame beneath my mask. I also sweat beneath my mask because guess what? THIS MASK IS FREAKING HOT! (Seriously, you know that guy who played Worf on *Star Trek: The Next Generation*? Well, he should have definitely received a special Oscar for having to endure so much alien sweatiness.)

Meanwhile, Mummy Quark keeps searching for Scout, in spite of the fact that his neck motion is compromised by all those bandages.

That's when it hits me. The answer to my prayer. I can fulfill my sacred vow by bringing Quark and Scout together.

Tonight.

I weave my way through the crowd until I am at Quark's side.

"Don't worry about anything," I whisper into his left bicep. "I'm here for you."

"Mmmmmmmmmmmm," says Quark.

The doorbell rings again. Ali magically materializes and greets his new guests—*Senhor Rick* and Ellie's aunt Mary.

"It's the Governator!" I make gargling noises to express my EXTREME agitation in my native tongue, Klingon.

"Rick! I haven't seen you at the gym lately," I hear Ali say as Quark and I scurry away. . . .

Scout's Take

"OH MY GOSH," I shout to Ellie over the music in Ali's living room. "Look who just walked through the door!"

Ellie squints. "The guy from *Star Trek*?"

"It's Ed. And I'll bet the mummy is his neighbor Quark."

Ellie squints. "How can you tell?"

"I'd know Ed's shuffle anywhere."

Ellie giggles. "Why are they dressed up?"

"You know Ed. Mr. Identity Crisis."

"Should we go over and say *alô*?" Ellie asks, apparently ready to forgive and forget. Amazing!

Just seeing Ed all dressed up like Worf, shifting nervously from one foot to the other, fills me with familiar fondness, and I realize I don't hate him anymore. Not that I ever really did.

On the other hand, it might not be a bad idea to let him suffer a little bit longer. Characters are always suffering in romance novels and it usually turns out to be good for them. Take Mr. Darcy in *Pride and Prejudice*, for example. Suffering made him stop being such a snob.

"Let's wait," I say, pulling Ellie into the hallway with me. I'm certain Ed and Quark haven't seen us yet, and for now, at least, I want to keep it that way.

Ellie and I drift through the kitchen and into the backyard, which is also jammed with people. Baskets of tumbling red and purple flowers hang from the branches of trees, while paper bags weighted with sand and filled with lit candles line the patio. Dragonflies flit by on stained-glass wings. The sweet-scented evening air hangs over us like a canopy.

Ellie breathes deeply.

"Honeysuckle and white nicotiana," she says. "Night bloomers. My grandmother grows them."

In the middle of the lawn, tables spread with linens are loaded with food: stuffed mushrooms, pasta salads, shrimp pink as roses, scallops sheathed in bacon, thin crackers and marbled cheeses, dips with meaty chunks of artichokes, chips and thick mango salsa, cream cheese and lemon tarts, bowls of brown sugar and bowls of sour cream speckled with orange rind, strawberries swirled in chocolate and mounded raspberries on chilled pewter platters.

Ellie's eyes grow large. "Wow!"

"I'm glad you approve," says Ali, coming up behind us. "The Warrior Princess and I try to make this evening a special one for friends and friends of friends."

We turn in time to see Ali give us a Cheshire smile before slipping into the crowd like the moon slipping behind the clouds.

Suddenly my chest feels full and light with gratitude for all the amazing things around me—food, music, dragonflies, flowers, the smell of flowers, bright lights and colored candles, happy people happy to be here, the warm midsummer night's air, the moon high and shining.

And most of all I am grateful for the person who would care enough to create such a night for his friends and the friends of his friends.

"I love you, Ali!" I blurt after him, completely surprised that I am saying such an outrageous, initmate thing but realizing too that I have never meant it more than at this very moment.

Ellie gives me a quick hug. She doesn't have to say it, but I know what has happened.

Her heart has been surprised by happiness too.

ED'S TURN

Time to spring into action here. My Springing-into-Action Plan involves looking for the object of Quark's desire and staying the hell away from Arnold S.

"Let's go find Scout," I say to Quark with nobleness.

The nobleness part is completely wasted on him though. He's already making a beeline for the backyard without me.

"Fine!" I shout after him. "Be that way! All you mummies are alike." Then I follow him like the angry Klingon that I am.

After accidentally walking into a broom closet or two, Quark and I finally find Scout and Ellie in the backyard. They're laughing and talking and nibbling on crackers like they don't have a care in the world.

Quark takes a step toward them, but I grab his arm. "Wait. Let's make a plan."

Quark hesitates. Can it be he's actually going to listen to me again? What should I tell him?

I stand in the shadows with Quark like a Klingon spy, mulling things over and watching the girls. Actually, I'm just pretty much watching Scout and the way her thick curly hair spills over her strong brown shoulders and the way she smiles and bites into a brownie with so much frosting that she has to lick her lips.

I almost stop breathing because I keep thinking how much I want to take her and lick all that chocolate right off those very full lips myself. . . .

I think of Quark and smack myself upside the head because a sacred vow is a sacred vow, and (as everybody knows) a Klingon is bound by honor to do the right thing.

Scout's Take

"The mummy is over there in the bushes watching you," Ellie says. "And so is Ed. You're the most popular girl at the party!"

My heart skips a quick beat as a slow smile grows across Ellie's face.

"Do you like Ed? Tell me the truth," she says.

I don't answer but my face gives me away.

"I knew it!" She laughs. "I suspected something after I told you I liked Sergio."

Still I say nothing.

"What's the matter, Scout?" Ellie asks.

"I'm afraid." There. I've said it. Out loud. For the first time ever. No taking the words back now.

"What are you afraid of?"

"Oh. You know. Ed's my best friend. What if I screw up our friendship?" Like an icy hand, fear touches my throat.

Ellie thinks this over. "That could happen, I guess. Life gets complicated whenever you love someone else."

The hand grows tighter. . . .

"I've made mistakes, Scout," Ellie says slowly. "I've even made the same mistake twice. But I honestly hope that won't stop me from falling in love again."

Coming from Ellie, this truly makes me want to cry. The music around us grows louder, making the leaves in the trees above our heads sway like dancers. Ellie takes my hand and I look at her.

"If you fail you fail. Meanwhile, you won't lose the kisses that are meant for you. Don't be afraid, Scout. Don't be afraid."

ED'S TURN

I CANNOT BELIEVE HOW FREAKING BLIND I'VE BEEN.

How could I have gone to work day after day after day and not seen Scout's magic? How did I get THAT so wrong too?

I want her, okay? But I cannot want her because I cannot have her because Quark wanted her before I did, which means he gets her, which means she'll spend the rest of her life (and mine) belonging to another man.

Wait a minute. That sounds like a bad movie script. Not even a bad movie script. A bad daytime TV script. Full of clichés and stuff. But you get the idea.

MEMO TO ED: You already screwed Quark over

once. You cannot and will not do it again.

"Stay here," I say to Quark. I can tell that fear of initiating contact with the female of the species is making him momentarily docile.

Time to put my little plan into action. Time to turn into Cyrano and woo Roxanne.

Scout's Take

"Tell me about Ed. What's he like in real life?" Ellie asks as she bites into a chocolate strawberry. We're now sitting together on a hammock strung between trees.

"He's smart. Funny. And in spite of the rotten thing he did to you, he can be very kind when he isn't mixed up about who he is."

Ellie thinks this over. "For example?"

"He makes it a point to talk to my grandfather the family outcast, for example, whenever he sees him sitting alone at one of my soccer games."

"Ed does have a great smile," Ellie says.

"Yup," I agree.

"And hair."

"That too."

The hammock swings gently—to and fro, to and fro.

"What about his friend?" Ellie asks.

"Quark? I don't know him that well. But he's nice. Really nice."

"Nice is good." Ellie gives Quark a long second look. Then she laughs. "Ed's on his way over here, although he keeps glancing over his shoulder."

"He's probably trying to stay off Ali's radar." Suddenly I feel as giddy as a romance-novel heroine. "Let's pretend we still don't notice him."

Ellie nods, then points. "Look who else is here. Mary and Rick!"

She waves. Mary and Rick wave back, and I think how strange it is that we're all connected. The world is just so small, really—as small as an oyster.

"You're on your own, lover girl," Ellie says. She threads her way through the crowd to join her aunt.

"Excuse me." Ed is at my side now, trying to disguise his voice. He doesn't sound very Worf-ly. I don't let him know that I know who he is and that I have always known who he is.

"Hi," I say, looking up at him from the hammock. "Great party, right?"

Ed grunts.

"I'm Scout, by the way. And you are?"

Pause. "Worf."

"Ah," I say.

"I have a friend who admires you very much," Ed/Sergio/Worf says.

Could he be talking about himself? Again, that spark of hope lights inside of me.

"A *friend*? Do I happen to know this *friend*?"

"He tells me you've met him a couple of times. Once in the library. Once at the place where you work."

Confused, I look at Ed/Sergio/Worf.

"My friend wants to get to know you better," he says. "I think you might like him. He's tall for his age."

Ed practically chokes on his own words as I (sort of) begin to understand. Quark. Ed is talking about Quark.

Quark?!!!! Has a crush on me?

Whereas yesterday this information might have made me cry, tonight it makes me laugh. Out loud. Ellie is right. Life is just too complicated for words. Complicated and funny and delicious.

Don't be afraid.

Suddenly I'm on the high dive again, just like in my dream, peeking past my toes into the deep, beautiful blue of the water below. This time I jump.

"I'm sure your friend is nice," I say slowly, "but actually I prefer men who are short."

I hear a quick intake of air through the mask. Is Ed excited? Or is he just suffocating?

"You do?"

"Yes," I say. "I do."

I see Ed hiding behind his silly mask, and suddenly I realize that I have been hiding too. I have been hiding from myself because the truth is that while I am a girl who kicks butt on and off the soccer field, I am also a girl with deep romance in my soul. I am Aurora Aurelia Arrington and I am not afraid.

I turn my full gaze on Ed and let it linger lovingly on his Klingon ears. Then I part my mouth and run the tip of my tongue over my lips, after which I say, "Let me tell you about this short guy I work with." I laugh a throaty laugh full of implication as I swing lazily in the hammock.

Ed stands there, rooted to the spot. Finally he says, "Will you excuse me for a minute please?"

He turns around and heads straight for the house, crashing like a bowling ball into everyone who gets in his way.

ED'S TURN

"Excuse me," I say to the person I have just bowled over, although what I really want to say is, "Did you hear what Scout just told me? She likes short guys!"

Short guys! As in Ed "Get Shorty" McIff. She likes us. She likes me.

ME!

She likes me me me me me me me me!

Did I already mention that Scout likes me?

So what am I going to do? What is Quark going to do? What am I going to do with Quark and what's he going to do with me? What's he going to do TO me?

One thing's for sure. I gotta get out of here right

now so I can think straight. And breathe straight too. It's getting harder to breathe with this stupid mask on. Time to take it off.

I should have taken it off a long time ago.

Scout's Take

Ali looks like he's hovering in midair, although he's just standing on a picnic table.

"May I have everyone's attention please?" he says in his deep rolling voice.

As if on cue, everybody in the house comes surging outside to join the rest of us standing beneath the flower-filled trees and strands of twinkling lights. Ed looks like he's trying to find a way to escape—tugging on Quark's bandaged arm and pointing back at the house. But in the end he gives it up. Meanwhile, the crowd gathers round to hear Ali speak in reverent tones.

"May I present to you your hostess for this evening—the Warrior Princess."

The crowd parts and the single most gorgeous woman I have ever seen appears among us, walking slowly and surely with regal, even steps toward Ali. She is tall and sleek with black-gold skin. Her hair and eyes are tawny, and she wears a gold halter top and tight leopard-skin pants. A blue parrot, the color of hyacinths, rides on her shoulder.

Gasps of admiration and awe follow as the Warrior Princess joins Ali on the table and takes his hand. She smiles at him and turns to the rest of us standing below.

"Thank you all for coming, friends and friends to be," she says in a low smoky voice. "And now let us have a song for Midsummer's Eve."

"A song! A song!" The crowd chants. "Who has a song?"

"Ellie does!" It's Rick, taking Ellie by the shoulders and pushing her forward. Mary smiles and claps her hands.

I would die a thousand slow and painful deaths if someone volunteered me to sing in front of strangers, but the look on Ellie's face says that she's pleased as she makes her way through the crowd. Ali and the Warrior Princess step down from the table so that Ellie can take their place. With a little smile and a slight nod of the head—first to the Warrior Princess and Ali and then to the crowd—Ellie says, "It will give me great pleasure to sing for you an aria from the opera *La Wally*."

She looks down. Clears her throat. Throws back her head.

She is shining. Her hair, her face, her skin. Right before our very eyes, she has transformed into someone else—someone wonderful and otherworldly. She opens her beautiful mouth and releases the first notes of a song as though they were birds. The sound of them is so rich and full, it almost breaks my heart.

This thought comes to me as I stand there watching and listening to Ellie—that a voice like hers, giving sound and shape to a songwriter's dreams, is the purest form of earthly magic.

Ellie's voice continues to weave itself around us all, and as I keep on listening, I realize my impression of a moment ago—that Ellie has turned into someone other than herself—was dead wrong. The real truth is that when Ellie sings, she is her deepest, truest self.

The crowd in Ali's backyard stands hypnotized. No one moves.

Except for Quark.

From where I am, I can see him frantically ripping the bandages from his face so that he can see better and hear better too. His mouth is wide open and his handsome eyes (they *are* handsome, even if they aren't my type of handsome) are as wide as skies.

At last (but too soon!) Ellie finishes.

The crowd erupts into cheers, and Ellie surveys us,

blushing with pride and pleasure.

And then . . .

She sees the Quark beneath the bandages.

Their eyes lock and *ZAP*!

Okay. I am here to bear witness. The charge of electricity that flies between those two is so potent and so real it absolutely singes the hair of those of us standing in its path.

Ellie is still throwing off sparks when she rejoins me.

"Do you believe in love at first sight?" she asks, her skin glowing beneath the lights.

I think about this. "I believe it's possible to see someone familiar with fresh eyes, which is like seeing them for the first time. Does that count?"

"Yes," she says as she looks at Quark. "That counts."

Ellie smiles and gives my arm a quick squeeze, then walks confidently toward Quark. For a split second I feel really and truly afraid for her heart. What if she gets hurt all over again? Let's be honest here. Her romance track record does not exactly inspire confidence.

I glance at Quark, who looks like one of those people from Pompeii who got frozen in time when Vesuvius erupted. The expression on his face is half terrified, half hopeful.

I know exactly how he feels.

And suddenly I feel better.

FROM THE LAB BOOK OF
QUENTIN ANDREWS O'ROURKE

WHEN FIRST I HEARD HER
By Quentin Andrews O'Rourke

When first I heard her
It was as though the moon
Had called out my name
At last.

She was bright above us
And it was as though
I had come home
At last.

(NOTE: It is acceptable for poems not to rhyme.)

The Letter Ellie Wrote

Dear Mom and Grandma,
I have never been happier. Details to follow!
Love from Ellie (who is over the moon)

THE EMAIL ELLIE WANTED TO SEND

(Um. There isn't one. . . .)

ED'S TURN

OUCH!

Whoa! Whatever current just passed between Quark and Elli practically blasts me off my feet. In fact, I sort of feel the way I did that time I plugged in the Christmas tree lights and blew them all out. Quark heads straight for me like a heat-seeking missile.

"Ed!" He yodels. "Did you hear that?"

I nod.

"Who *is* she?"

I grin as I explain. Frankly it doesn't take a genius to see that as far as Quentin Andrews O'Rourke is concerned, Scout (who prefers short men) is ancient Egyptian history.

Yes!

Not that I deserve this kind of help from the universe, but, *yes again!*

"Go talk to her," I say to Quark, who is suddenly suffering from an acute case of rigor mortis. I give him a little shove. "You can do it."

Without any particular plan of attack in mind, I thread my way through the crowd toward Scout.

"I'm back," I say.

"So I see."

"I have something to tell you."

"So tell me."

I clear my throat. "I am tired of disguises. I am tired of deceptions."

"Me too."

"And besides that, I can't breathe."

Scout laughs as I lift the mask off my head and come face-to-face with her.

"I am not Sergio who surfs off the coast of Australia," I say.

"Or hunts big game in Canada with Canadian Mounties," she says.

"Or races Formula One cars and frolics with topless princesses in Monaco," I say.

"Or rides camels in Egypt."

"Or hikes in the Himalayas," I say. "I'm Ed. Who sweats."

The two of us look straight at each other and laugh again, and this time we cannot stop laughing, even when everyone around us starts to dance.

I'm not kidding. They're all dancing. The kids and the ladies with the dogs, the Goths, the skaters, the guy with the snake, the moms in the sweatsuits, T. Monroe, Rick and Mary, Quark and Ellie, Ali and the Warrior Princess. Dancing and spinning and swirling, they sweep us through Ali's house with them out onto Fourth Avenue and across the street into the old Salt Lake Cemetery, where beneath a bright moon, shadows leap happily out of the ground to join us.

"Look at all these people," breathes Scout, "dancing on graves."

"Dancing on graves?" I say. "What a great cliché!"

Then I pull Scout tight against me and we join them—hand in hand we dance by the light of the moon.

Scout's Take

You are NOT going to believe what just happened!

As Ed and I were dancing, we accidentally collided with an older couple dancing next to us.

"Sorry about that!" Ed apologized immediately.

I recognized the woman. She comes into Reel Life with her two little granddaughters, Maria and Rosa, whom Ali entertains with magic tricks.

"No problem," her partner said. He gave us a gentle smile and held out a calloused hand—a strong hand that has known years of hard work—and said, "I'm Sergio and this is Pilar, my good wife of forty summers and counting. Pleased to meet you."

I gasped. Ed practically swallowed his own teeth. "You're Sergio?"

He nods.

"Did you ever work at Reel Life?"

Again, the true Sergio nods.

"Dude! I've been wearing your badge, like, forever!"

The true Sergio laughed. "I worked there a long time ago. Ali hired me when Pilar was ill and I was between jobs. Ali is a good friend, is he not?"

Ed nodded slowly, then clasped Sergio's outheld hand. "I'm Ed McIff, and this is Aurora Aurelia Arrington." He turned to me with a dazzling smile. "My girlfriend of one summer evening . . . and counting."

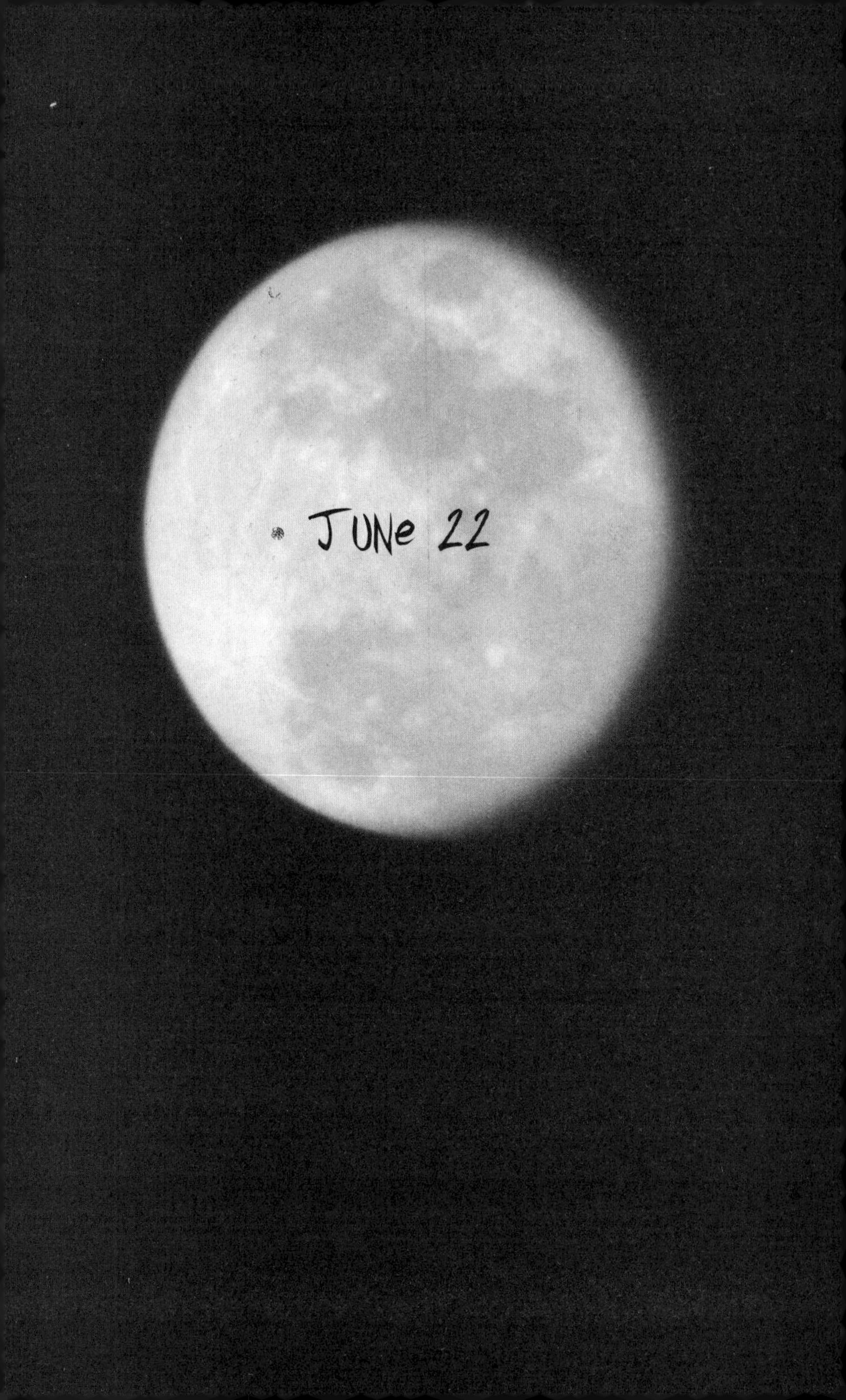
JUNE 22

EPILOGUE

The next day at work Ali says, "I got something for you, McIff. Here."

He drops a brand-new badge on the counter in front of me. It says "Ed."

I pick up my name tag and turn it over a couple of times in my hands. "Finally."

Ali shoots me a wicked grin. "Had to make you earn it first."

Carefully he removes the name tag that says "Sergio" from my frilly shirt and banks that baby straight into the garbage can.

"So long, farewell, *auf Wiedersehen*, good-bye," I say, channeling Maria von Trapp.

He watches as I put on the new one, after which he gives me a casual salute. I snap to attention like John Wayne in an old war movie and start to sing loudly. "Silver wings upon their chest! These are men, America's best!"

Ali immediately puts me in a choke hold. "You one crazy mother, McIff. You know that?"

"I know that," I say, happy that I am a crazy mother.

Ali releases me, plants a friendly slug on my arm, and strolls toward his office.

Had to make you earn it first. Ali's words run suddenly through my head like the lyrics of a song so good it gives you goose bumps.

I call him out just before he steps into his office. "ALI!"

He turns around slowly, folding his great thick arms across his great thick chest. The hoops in his ears gleam gold.

"Yeah?"

I try to put into words the brand-new, incredibly insane thought that I'm thinking. "Did you—did you set me up? Did you give me Sergio's name *on purpose*?"

Ali throws back his head and roars out a huge laugh that hangs in the air above us like the smile of a crescent moon.

Then he turns around and disappears into his office without saying a word.

Poof!